Surging Tide

Cottage by the Sea Series, Volume 1

Lexy Timms

Published by Dark Shadow Publishing, 2022.

SURGING TIDE

First edition. January 30, 2022.

Written by Lexy Timms.

The Sea Cottage Series #1
SURGING
TIDE
USA TODAY BESTSELLING AUTHOR
LEXY TIMMS

The Sea Cottage Series #1
SURGING
TIDE
USA TODAY BESTSELLING AUTHOR
LEXY TIMMS

Surging Tide

The Sea Cottage Series #1

Cover by: Book Cover by Design[1]

1. http://bookcoverbydesign.co.uk/

The Sea Cottage Series

Surging Tide
Distant Shores
Twisting Ocean

Find Lexy Timms:

Lexy Timms Newsletter:
https://www.lexytimms.com/newsletter
Lexy Timms Facebook Page:
https://www.facebook.com/LexyTimmsAuthor
Lexy Timms Website:
http://www.lexytimms.com

Want to read more...
For **FREE**?
Sign up for Lexy Timms' newsletter
And she'll send you updates on new releases, ARC copies of books and a whole lotta fun!
Sign up for news and updates!
https://www.lexytimms.com/newsletter

Surging Tide Blurb

Sometimes, one must go against the tide...

Gabriella – Gabby for short – desperately needs a holiday. She's worked way too hard, just lost her father and wants a break. From everything. She books a stay at a picturesque cottage by the sea. No phone, no internet, no neighbors – just books, a bottle of wine and the beach. A month without distraction and a chance to find herself again.

Until a hunk of a guy suddenly shows up catching her sunbathing in her birthday suit. The man is hot as sin. Jake Wolfe is cocky and stubborn too.

Double booked. Double trouble.

Stuck on an island with a stranger, they try to make the best of it, but get on each other's nerves. When a drunken night leads to steamy passion, they realize something's brewing, and like the unpredictability of stormy weather, things could get rough.

SURGIN
TIDE
LEXY TIMM
SURGING
TIDE
LEXY TIMMS
GET IT ON
Google Play
kobo
Available at
amazon
nook

Chapter One

Gabby

"Incoming!" I heard the head trauma nurse call out.

We were ready. I was already dressed in my gown with my gloves on. "Bring him in," I said calmly as the paramedics rolled a patient into Trauma One. From the moment I laid eyes on my patient, I was already assessing him. I listened to the medics spout out his vitals and pertinent information.

I stepped to the side of the bed as he was transferred from the gurney to our hospital bed. The adrenaline I'd felt dissipated. This man was not critical. He was bloodied from a cut on his head, but he was looking directly at me.

"You're going to be fine," I told him, and gently patted his arm. "We're going to check you from tip to top to be sure. What happened?"

"Skateboarding," he said with a cocky smile.

I nodded as I tapped against his belly. "You were knocked out?"

"That's what my buddy says." He grimaced when I touched the arm that was obviously broken. "He got it all on video. I can't wait to see it. I bet it's going to go viral. I'm going to be a star."

I studied his face, which was covered with blood, and cocked my head to the side. "I've seen you before, haven't I?"

"Yes, ma'am." He grinned and flashed teeth stained with his own blood. "I'd never forget the face of the hottest doctor in LA."

It wasn't exactly the first time I'd been hit on while at work. I was one of the younger doctors in the ED and young men – usually young, but there'd been a few older guys that seemed to forget their manners – liked to flirt. I rarely paid much attention to the compliments. Often, patients were already hopped up on pain meds by the time I saw them. Delirious with pain, shock, and pharmaceuticals.

"All right, Casanova," I said. "Don't move, and let me check you out."

"Check me out, doc." He grinned.

After quickly assessing his injuries, I stepped back and gave out orders to the nurses. The man looked fine and didn't require my attention. I was off work in ten minutes. He would be passed off to the next doctor while all the tests I ordered were being run. I stepped out of the room while the nurses took care of him and ordered the x-rays he would need to be cleared.

"I thought that was going to be a bad one," Tammy, the head nurse, said from behind the desk.

"Me too." I nodded. "All that blood. It always looks bad."

"The paramedics called it in as a priority," she said. "Sorry to get your blood pumping only to be disappointed."

I laughed as I recorded the information on the man's digital chart. "Trust me, I'm not disappointed to have gotten an easy case. A complicated trauma would not get me out of here on time."

"You're never out of here on time," she laughed.

"I am today," I said. "I've actually got plans.

"Are you really going to leave on time?" she asked with feigned shock.

"I hope so," I said, and checked the clock. "Assuming no one else comes through that door."

"Keep your fingers and toes crossed," she laughed. "You know it never works out that way."

"I know, but today, I need it to. I am already dreaming of a sandy beach with the sun beating down on my naked body. I won't have a waiter to deliver me drinks, but I'll pretend I'm sipping a Mai Tai."

"Dr. Kingston!" she exclaimed. "You naughty, naughty girl."

"It's about time I was naughty," I said with my stylus in hand. I was scanning the charts of the patients still in the ED. "I need this vacation. If I don't unwind, I'm seriously going to explode."

"It's been too long," she said. "I'm glad you're getting some time. Where are you going? You said it was somewhere very private."

I looked up and grinned. "Very, very private. It's an island off the coast of Maine. It's totally off the grid and rustic. I'm not taking my cell. Nothing. No internet. No TV. Nothing."

She looked horrified. "Why in the world would you do that?"

"Because I need to unplug and reset," I told her. "I've been busting my ass for thirty of my thirty-four years. It's been ten years since I took any kind of vacation. I'm so ready to curl up with a book and listen to the ocean. No background noise. No sirens. No one paging me. Just blissful peace."

"How long are you going to be there?" she asked.

This was the part I knew would really freak her out. "I reserved the cottage for a month."

Her eyes damn near popped out of her head. "A month! You're going to go a month without your cell phone?"

"Yes." I nodded. "I might get tired of the quiet after a week or two and go into town, but I don't think I will. I really need this time. It's been—" I stopped short of telling her why I wanted to get away. "I need it."

"You're the hardest working doctor in this hospital," she said with a smile. "You deserve it. We'll miss you around here."

"I'll miss you, and I'll probably miss the job, but all I can think about is getting out of here."

"Is it a legit private island?" she asked. "Like, you're going to be out there all by yourself?"

"Yes." I grinned. "Complete solitude."

"How are you going to eat?" she asked. "Drink? What are you going to do for a month?"

"There's a guy that brings groceries once a week," I explained. "I already did my grocery order."

"But what if you need to run to the store for something?" she asked. "What if you get hurt and need help? What if you get sick?"

"You sound like a very overprotective mother," I teased. "If I need anything, I'll figure out how to do without. If I get sick, I'll ride it out. I'm a doctor. I'm healthy. There is an emergency flare I can shoot up if the island sinks or something like that."

"I always suspected you were just a little off," she laughed. "Only you could think deserting yourself on an island would be a good time."

"The best time," I said.

"Have you ever done that before?" she asked. "Gone off into the wild by yourself?"

"No," I said with a shake of my head. "That's why I'm so excited to do it. It's a new adventure."

"A new adventure is moving to a new city or taking a new job," she joked. "You're going off the grid in every sense of the word. You're a city girl. You've been born and raised in the city. How are you going to survive?"

"You're making it sound like I'm going to live in a tent on a deserted island. It's a house, cottage rather. Running water, electricity, food, and everything I need. Most of all, privacy. Complete, total privacy."

"All right, all right," she said with her hands up. "I won't bug you about your very unconventional vacation choices. Are you at least going to take your cell phone in case of emergency?"

"Nope." I smiled. "No service."

"What about taking pictures?" she asked. "You have to take some pictures of this place."

"I don't know," I shrugged. "I might. I think part of the beauty of it is the fact you can only remember it. You don't get pictures. If I want to remember it, I'll have to close my eyes to do it."

"I suppose," she said with a shake of your head. "It's your show."

"Thank you. I will try and get a picture of the place, but I'm not going to take hundreds."

She walked around the desk and gave me a hug. "All right. You do whatever you have to. Have fun. It is kind of exciting that you're doing what suits you and no one else. Take care of yourself."

I finished up with my charts, checked on the skateboarding kid and declared myself officially off duty. As I walked to the parking garage, I felt free. I was officially on vacation. It had been way too long since I took any real time off. Too long since I did something for me and me alone. This was the first time I was taking time off work to actually just do nothing at all.

I couldn't wait to be on the beach on the other side of the country. California had amazing beaches, but there were people everywhere. I couldn't wait to be alone. Most people went on vacation and visited touristy hotspots. Not me. I saw people all day every day. Usually, I met people on their worst days. It was rarely pleasant. Ten years of working in the emergency department of a busy hospital as an intern and through residency had taken a toll. The constant pain and suffering and even death weighed on me like a heavy cloak. I had to find a way to get rid of it or I was going to burn out before I reached my thirty-fifth birthday.

I took off my white coat and tossed it in the backseat of my car before getting behind the wheel and heading home to my two-bedroom condo. One day I was going to buy a house out of the city, but for now, it was the condo. The only reason I was able to afford the place was because of my inheritance from my parents.

I walked at a fast clip through the lobby and hopped on the elevator. I was already thinking about what I needed to do. I wasn't leaving until first thing in the morning. I needed to pack and clean up. Tomorrow was going to be a long day and I wanted to be well rested. I was coming off a thirty-six-hour shift and needed to catch up on some sleep. I would sleep on the plane as well.

"Alexa, what's the weather like in coastal Maine?" I asked as I kicked off my shoes.

I listened to the forecast and smiled. It was going to be beautiful this time of year. Early summer with hopefully no chance of violent storms. I was used to being on my own and doing things for myself, but even I was a little afraid of Mother Nature. Being alone on a somewhat deserted island with no connection to the outside world was enough of a challenge.

I stripped out of the clothes I'd been wearing for almost two days and tossed them on the floor to deal with later. I needed a shower. I stepped into my modern shower with high water pressure and wondered what it was going to be like to go primitive. The cottage had running water and solar electricity with a generator for backup. I had searched for the right place and while there were plenty of bigger and more luxurious places, I had chosen the little one-bedroom cottage.

I stepped out of the shower and dressed in my usual sleep pants and threw on a shirt before I started a load of laundry. That was going to be the tricky thing about the cabin. There weren't any laundry facilities. I was going to be there for a month, which meant I had to pack enough clothes to last a month without completely stinking myself up. The owner of the cottage advised I go into town once a week with the grocery delivery man, but I didn't want to leave the island. I would wash my clothes in the sink if I had to. Considering I was going to be on a private island, clothing was optional anyway.

I started a load of laundry and then got busy packing. I didn't need a bunch of fancy outfits. Bikinis, shorts, and tees were going to be my attire for the next thirty days. I threw in a couple of sweaters for cool nights and then packed my toiletries bag.

"Anything else?" I asked aloud. "What am I forgetting?"

I scanned my bedroom and tried to think of what else I might need. There was nothing. This was a very stripped-down vacation. I only needed the essentials. I left my bags by the front door and after finishing up cleaning my apartment, I headed for bed. I was so excited for tomorrow. I was anxious to be alone, even though I was alone most of the time. The island was going to be a different kind of alone.

It was probably silly, but I felt like I had to center myself. I felt adrift. I needed to take a timeout from life and get my head straight. Everyone I worked with would never know I was in an internal battle. Things in my life were great to anyone looking at it from the outside. I was good at hiding my feelings. I was great at plodding along and pretending everything was all right.

"Go to sleep," I told myself.

I closed my eyes and tried like hell to sleep. My brain was moving a million miles a minute. I was going through my travel list, thinking about the patients I'd seen over the last two days, and imagining the cottage and the quiet. All simultaneously. I had the proverbial hamster wheel going in my head. Despite the pre-vacation jitters, I was smiling. It was the first time I had truly smiled in weeks.

"This is going to be so good," I whispered.

Chapter Two

Jake

I stared at the wall across from my desk. There was a painting of the ocean by some famous painter. I didn't know who. I focused on the lighthouse as my lawyer droned on. And on and on. When I heard enough of the man's lecturing, I cut him off.

"Jim, I appreciate your concern, but I don't care about the house," I spoke into the air. My lawyer was on speaker, freeing up my hands to write down the list of things I needed to pack when I got home.

"Jake, we're talking about a lot of money here," he said.

"Yep, and it sucks, but I'll make more. I have enough."

"Why don't you let me force her into selling the house?" he said. "She'll have to split the proceeds."

"I'm sure once she's married, she will sell the house," I said dryly. "I'll get my money then."

"She's living in your house with another man," he reminded me.

It wasn't like I forgot. How could I? "What's your point, Jim?"

"My point is you have a lot to argue with here. You don't have to give up half of everything."

"I don't want to see her again," I said. "I don't want to keep paying you five-hundred bucks an hour to get screwed. She's doing a great job of that on her own. I need this behind me so I can move past this disaster that is my life. That woman took fifteen years of my life. I'm so over it. I want it over. She can marry whoever she wants. I'm just glad I got out of paying alimony."

"Barely," he muttered. "You're absolutely sure you want me to file it like this?"

"Yep," I replied. "I'm tired of fighting. She's destroyed me. Now it's time for me to put the pieces back together."

"Okay," he sighed. "I'll get it done today."

"Thank you," I said. "Jim, no offense but I really hope we never have to see each other again."

His laughter echoed around my office. "What are you going to do now?" he asked.

"I'm going on vacation."

"Good," he said. "Good for you. It's been a long year. You need a break. Where are you going? Cancun? Hawaii?"

"Actually, no," I said and looked at the image on my computer. "I'm going far enough away no one can call me or find me. Not you, and definitely not Amanda."

"Where are you headed?" he asked.

I grinned and stared at the picture on my screen. "A private island."

"Shit, I guess I don't have to worry about your finances," he joked.

"You don't have to worry about my finances, but it's not that kind of island. It's a simple, somewhat rustic cottage. I plan on doing nothing but fishing, swimming, drinking, and absolutely nothing else. I'm not going to work. I won't be networking or talking to anyone. In fact, I'll be totally off the grid."

There was a long silence. "You're going to do this little Zen retreat for how long?"

"A month," I told him.

"You're going off the grid for an entire month?" he repeated. "What about the business?"

"I haven't been hands-on in the business for over a year now," I told him. "When Amanda walked out, I walked away. I've got a good management team in place. They don't need me."

"Where is this place?" he asked. "Just in case I have to send out the Coast Guard."

"Somewhere off the coast of Maine," I answered.

"Does it have a private airstrip?"

"Nope," I said. "A boat. A single boat will ferry me out and bring me necessities once a week."

"No shit!" he exclaimed. "You're going to be that alone?"

"Yep. And I cannot wait. I'm driving out tomorrow."

"Okay. Good luck, and I'm sorry things worked out the way they did," he said.

"I'm not," I said with a shrug. "I'm glad it's over."

I ended the call and clicked off the website with the cottage info. Amanda would die if she knew what I was going to do. My ex-wife was pampered and spoiled. I'd been a part of her world for too long. When we met, she captivated me. The beautiful young woman who was fresh out of college and working at a financial firm. I was a kid, barely twenty, fresh off an Olympic bronze win with money in my pocket. She had just gotten a job at a financial firm. I hired her as my financial advisor. Then we started dating and before I knew it, we were married.

I started making money at my sporting goods store. Then I opened another and another. The more money I made, the happier she seemed to be to spend it. When we first got married, there was talk about starting a family and moving out of New York City. We made it about an hour north and that was it. She kept me in the city. She put off the family thing because she wasn't ready. The more money I made, the less happy I became. Not her, though. She seemed to be finding her stride while I felt like I was suffocating. Apparently, she didn't like my desire to slow down and get away from the social scene.

I shook my head as I walked out of the office in my home. That memory was forever burned into my brain.

I had walked into our big ass house – too big for just two people – and went upstairs. And there she was, naked as the day she'd been born. At first, I was stupid enough to think she was surprising me. Then the man walked out of the bathroom behind her. To her credit, it was the same man she was living with now. In my house.

I had packed my bags that day and never went back. I bought myself a nice house on some land in Maine and never looked back. I took my clothes, my car, my medal, and a few random trinkets. I walked away from my business as the acting leader and ran things from my house. This was the life I was supposed to have. I needed space and clean air. I was not a city boy. I was not the kind of guy who liked fancy dinners and the opera.

I was going to sleep under the stars on a sandy beach with no one around to bother me. I felt guilty for leaving my students behind, but they understood. I wasn't an official coach by any means. I was more of a mentor. I had always loved all aspects of track and field, but the javelin had been the one thing I excelled at. I would have won gold if it hadn't been for the damn rotator cuff injury. It was the same story that so many athletes got to tell.

So close, and yet so far. It was a reminder that we were all human. No matter how many hours we trained, we weren't invincible. Mentoring young athletes made me feel useful, and I had always hoped I would have my own son or daughter or both by my thirty-five. I wanted to teach my kids about all the stuff I loved. I wanted to teach them to fish and take them on overnight hiking trips, but I was afraid that dream was gone. I had wasted fifteen years of my life with the wrong woman. I had been burned and couldn't quite think of a future with another woman. No woman meant no kids.

While in my bedroom tossing things into my suitcase, my cell rang. I glanced down at the screen to see Amanda's name, and couldn't even begin to imagine what she wanted now. If I didn't answer, she would call a hundred times. I could shut off my phone but that would mean she won. I was about sick of the woman winning.

"What?" I snapped as I answered.

"My lawyer just called me," she said.

"Good for you. That probably cost you a few hundred."

"He told me your attorney just called him," she went on in that super irritating, condescending tone that I loathed.

"Is this a game of telephone?" I asked with a sigh. "Who should I call next?"

"You signed," she cooed.

"Whatever it takes to get you out of my life for good."

"Don't be like that, Jake," she said, and I could practically see her pout. Back in the beginning, I had thought that pout was so pretty. Whenever she wanted something, she would turn on her pout and I couldn't resist it. I hated it now. It made my skin crawl to know I had been so easily manipulated.

"What do you want, Amanda?" I asked with irritation. I imagined myself on that deserted island with no way for her to contact me. If I never heard her voice again, it would be too soon.

"I wanted to say I have a few boxes in the garage for you," she said.

"And you just now remembered?"

"No, I just wanted to make sure you would sign the papers," she said, as if her attempt to blackmail me wasn't a big deal.

"Burn it," I said. "I don't know what it is, and I don't care. I've lived this long without it, I don't need it now. Give it to Dale. He seems to like my hand-me-downs."

"Don't be a dick," she snapped.

"Burn it. Give it away. Drown it. I don't care. You got what you wanted. Have a great life, Amanda."

I ended the call. I no longer had to play nice. I didn't have to listen to her bullshit. She had nothing more over me. She couldn't bully me into anything ever again. It was over. Damn that felt good to say. "It's over!" I shouted into my bedroom.

This vacation was a celebration and a new beginning. Moving to Maine had been a good first step, but finalizing the divorce was what I really needed. This was the finality I needed to move forward with my life. I couldn't wait to be under the stars with zero light pollution. It was going to be just the ocean and the stars and me.

I grabbed the sleeping bag I purchased specifically for this trip. I had my fire starter, flashlight, and other essentials. The cottage was likely stocked with all the stuff I needed, but I didn't want to risk being without something important. I grabbed the brand-new fillet knife I had bought specifically for the trip. The cottage owner had promised me the place had all the fishing supplies I would need, and I could practically taste the pan-fried fish cooked over an open fire.

I loaded up my car in preparation for an early start. While I had already placed my grocery order, I was also bringing along some of the basics. I had a bottle of scotch I'd been saving for the day my divorce was finalized. Technically, we still had to wait on the judge, but for all intents and purposes, this was over. I could open my scotch while sitting in front of a fire on a beach far away from her and our old life.

I made myself a frozen meal and sat down in front of the TV. It was the last time I would be watching TV for a month. I wasn't going to miss it. I was going to leave my phone locked in my car. I wasn't taking my laptop, and was leaving my smartwatch behind as well. The new tactical watch I bought for the trip was all I needed.

Some people, including the COO at my company, thought I was crazy. To purposely strand myself on a deserted isle seemed like a drastic idea, but I was looking forward to it. My life had been nonstop from the moment I started walking. My parents saw an athlete in me and pushed me at every sport until it seemed running was my thing. Then, when I was ten, I was at a high school track meet and saw the javelin throw. I was intrigued and had to try it. From then on, it was nonstop training. I went to the Olympics at the age of nineteen and before I could compete in my second event, my shoulder gave up. That was it. My career was over.

Then there was Amanda and the business. Another fifteen years of busting ass to try and be good enough. When it became obvious I wasn't going to win the gold with her, it hurt. It stung. I hated the idea of failing. It took me a good six months after I left to realize I hadn't failed. She did; she quit, not me, and I was lucky she did. I saw that now, but it had taken a long time to get to this point.

Tomorrow was the first day of the rest of my life, and it couldn't come soon enough.

Chapter Three

Gabby

My alarm went off and I was out of bed like a shot. Today was the day, and I was giddy with excitement. I couldn't wait. I dressed, brushed my teeth and put on just a little makeup. The Uber was waiting for me outside. It was bright and early with most of the city still asleep, and within minutes, my bags were loaded and we were off to the airport. In eight hours, I would be on the beach.

After getting through security, I sat down and waited to board. I had my phone with me, but it wasn't on. Today I was officially on vacation and I didn't want to check email, the news, or my phone. I was in my own little bubble. I had three books with me, which I knew I would burn through in no time. The cottage owner promised a well-stocked bookshelf along with puzzles and cards for a little solitaire. I wasn't worried about being bored. I was looking forward to it.

While I waited, I watched the hustle and bustle of my fellow travelers. Everyone was in a hurry. Most of them looked like they were traveling for business. There were plenty of families heading out on vacation. I remembered those mornings when we would leave for vacation when I was younger. My parents would be on the phone the whole time. Each of them talking to their nurses and fellow doctors. While we were on vacation, they were still connected to their practices. We were out of town, but their hearts were still at home.

That was why I wanted to take a real vacation. My parents didn't know how to relax. I had picked up that trait, but after my father died last month, I realized life was short. He'd been seventy-nine, but he worked up until he was seventy-two. He retired and relaxed for a whole seven years. Seven years was not enough life. I wanted real living. I didn't want to be like my dad and look back on my life and thinking, 'Boy I sure worked a lot.' Granted, he'd saved countless lives, but at what cost to his own?

I heard my flight called and quickly grabbed my purse and carry-on. This was it. The flight was just under six hours. Then it was an hour's drive to the dock where I was supposed to meet the boat that would ferry me out to the island. Just thinking about a glass of wine while I watched the sunset was making me feel like I was going to spontaneously combust.

My plan had been to try and sleep a little on the plane to lessen the impact of the jetlag and to try and catch up on the months of no sleeping. I didn't want to spend my vacation sleeping. I was going to sleep in and take it easy, but I wanted to be present in the moment.

Six hours later, the plane landed at the small airport and I quickly found the Uber I had reserved days ago. I was a planner. I didn't want to get to the airport and waste time waiting around for a ride. The driver was waiting for me with a little sign. It was very cute and made me want to stay forever.

"Hello," I greeted him.

"You must be Miss Kingston," he said with a bright smile.

"That's me."

He took my bags and led me outside. The weather was similar to what I was used to in California, but the humidity was much higher. "You're here on vacation?" he asked.

"I am," I said as I got into the front seat of his car.

"Where are you from?"

"LA," I answered.

"Ah, one coast to the other," he laughed. "Is it different?"

"The ocean is on the other side," I joked.

"What brings you out to our little corner of the woods?" he asked.

"I'm on vacation," I told him. "I'm just hoping to slow down and enjoy the quiet."

"You'll definitely have that here," he said.

I wasn't going to tell a complete stranger I was going to be on a deserted island all by myself. I wasn't that naïve. I'd seen the results of women trusting men they didn't know and vice versa. I was not trying to find myself sliced and diced and tossed in the water.

He pulled up to a boat launch and parked. "Here?" he asked.

"Yes," I told him. "This is the place. I'm meeting a man here."

"Would you like me to wait with you?" he asked.

"Nah, I'm good, but thank you."

He insisted on carrying my bag to the single bench at the dock. I was expecting the dock to be busy with fishing boats, but there were a few trucks with trailers parked in the lot and nothing else. I hoped like hell I was in the right spot. The website said a man would be waiting to take me to the island. He was supposed to be wearing a neon orange shirt. So far, I saw no one matching that description. I hoped like hell I hadn't gotten scammed.

Soon enough, I saw a boat coming up to the dock. The man was wearing a neon orange shirt. It had to be him. I wasn't surprised to see the boat was nothing fancy. The website said it was a quaint ride, so I had lowered my expectations, but not quite this low. It made me nervous about what the cottage was going to look like. I prayed I hadn't been totally taken advantage of. I did not want to be one of those people writing about some horrible bait and switch experience.

With my suitcase trailing behind me and my carry-on slung over my shoulder, I made my way down to the dock. "Hello," I greeted him with a smile. "I'm Gabby. I believe I'm supposed to be meeting you."

"Hello, Gabby," the grizzled, bearded man returned. "Captain Oleg Macdonald at your service."

I shook his hand and let him take my bag. "It's a beautiful day," I commented.

"Yes, it is," he said, slightly out of breath as we walked towards the boat. "I delivered the groceries earlier. Do you want to take a minute to grab anything else?"

This was the moment. It was starting to sink in. I was about to desert myself on an island with no stores, no anything. What I had was what I had for the week. "Um, no thank you," I said. "I think I'm good. If not, I'll survive."

He chuckled and climbed into the boat before reaching for my bag. "If you need help, shoot up that flare. You might need to send up two. In the daylight, I won't see it. You're really on your own out there, but if there are plenty of fishermen that pass by this island who you can try and flag down if you need to. They'll radio me and I'll get out there as quickly as I can. I live right over there." He pointed to a tiny house not too far from the shoreline.

"I will do that, thank you," I said. He reached out and helped me onto the boat.

"You got some warm stuff in that bag?" he asked.

"Yes, why?"

"We get some cold nights when a storm kicks up," he said and moved to start the boat.

"Is it normally stormy this time of year?"

"It happens," he said with all the wisdom of a man who'd lived by the sea the bulk of his life.

He reminded me of an old sailor with the white beard and matching shock of hair. I wouldn't be the least bit surprised to discover he had a wooden leg. "I brought some warm clothes."

"Do you know how to start a fire if needed?" he asked over the sound of the engine.

"In a fireplace?" I asked.

"Yes. Just in case it gets chilly. There's already wood cut and stacked."

"I have started fires in the past," I told him. Although, it had been a long time since I'd had to do it. People accidentally started fires all the time. It couldn't be that hard.

"So, what brings you all the way out here to this little piece of nowhere?" he asked.

"Peace," I answered honestly. "I'm looking for a little peace and quiet."

He chuckled before bursting into a coughing fit. "You're going to find that here. Trust me. I've seen plenty of people come out here for a little getaway and not make it a full week. People are too used to the noise. They don't want it, but they can't live without it."

"You're probably not wrong, but I think I'll last longer than a week," I told him confidently. "I'm planning on staying the full month."

The boat bounced over the choppy water. My long, blonde hair was free and blowing in the wind. I always wore my hair up when I was at work. I was enjoying the freedom of it being loose. The wind burned my eyes, but I didn't look away. I could see an island in the distance. There were several technically, but I was certain that the one we were drawing close to was mine.

As the shoreline came into view, the excitement I'd been feeling all day ramped up. He slowed the boat and pulled up to an old wooden dock. "This is it," he said and cut the engine. I waited while he tied the boat up and climbed out. "Hand me your bag."

I tossed it up, along with my purse and other bag. He reached for my hand and once again helped me out of the boat. "Want me to walk you up to the cottage?" he asked.

"I'm good," I said with a bright smile. "At least I know I can't get lost on an island," I joked.

"Just follow that path up to the house," he said. "I'll be back on Friday. Again, if you need anything, shoot the flare. You might get a bar on your cell, but it isn't a guarantee."

"I'll be okay," I promised him. "Thank you for everything."

He hopped back into his boat. “Enjoy your time,” he said and gave me a wave.

I waved and watched him drift farther out in the water. “Yes!” I shouted at the sky.

I started up the path that was a combination of wood shavings and dirt. My suitcase bumped along behind me. I could see the little house through the trees and walked faster, pausing when the house came fully into view. I couldn’t stop smiling; it was perfect. The house was small with a small covered front porch, and two rockers sat on either side of the front door. It was so cute and welcoming.

I lifted the flowerpot and found the key just like the owner said. I quickly unlocked the door and pushed it open. The kitchen consisted of a single door fridge and one counter. The propane fueled stove sat against one wall with a wheeled island parked beside it. The place was small, but it was just me. I didn’t need big.

I checked out the single bedroom with a standard queen-size bed. The bathroom was across the small hall. All very standard and what you would expect to find in a standard hotel room. I didn’t bother unpacking. I left the suitcase on the bed and checked out the small pantry that had been locked. I assumed it was locked in case nosey intruders found the cottage while out exploring.

The refrigerator had all the stuff I had asked for and then some. I picked up the hard salami before putting it back in the fridge. That was definitely not on my list. I assumed it was the good captain improvising. There was a small liquor cabinet, also locked with the key stashed in the freezer. It was stocked with a little of everything. The wine I had requested and paid for was lined up on the counter next to the fridge. To the naked eye, I probably looked like a lush. I just wanted to make sure I didn’t run out.

I opened one of the bottles and poured myself a glass. “Officially on vacation,” I declared, and held up my glass.

I took a drink and looked out the large picture window that faced the water. The view was blocked a bit by the trees, but I could see it out there. I was a hundred percent alone. There was no one around for miles, which meant it was time to do the one thing I promised myself I would do. I kicked off my shoes and shimmied out of my shorts and panties. Then it was my shirt and bra. I laughed and opened the front door. I grabbed a towel from the bathroom, slid on my sunglasses, and walked down to the beach in all my naked glory. I spread out the towel just above the water's edge and stretched out. The sun beat down on my skin. The sound of the water gently lapping at the shore and birds screeching overhead surrounded me. It was like being transported away in a dream, except it was all real. This was better than any dream I had been having in anticipation of this day.

Chapter Four

Jake

I walked around the house, unplugging things just in case there was a power outage. I didn't want to fry my electronics. Basically, I was stalling. The boat guy wasn't meeting me until three. I locked all the windows and flopped down on the couch to wait.

My phone rang and I just knew I didn't want to look at the screen. I didn't have to guess who it was. It was a very special ringtone, an eerie tune. One that had been used in a horror film. I didn't bother reaching for the phone. She could leave a message. There was nothing I needed or wanted to say to my now ex-wife.

The call ended and a moment later it started ringing again. I reached for it and declined the call. Why didn't I just block her damn number? I wanted to, but I worried she would do something else to get to me. But then again, it was time to cut the cord. The phone rang again. I hit the beat it button. Then there was a text followed by another phone call.

"What?" I answered. "What could you possibly want from me? Haven't you taken everything? We're so over, Amanda. There's nothing more to say."

"You don't have to be so rude," she snapped.

"I think I have to be."

"Did you tell Phil Michelson I cheated on you?" she snapped.

I could not believe I was listening to this. "Amanda, why are you calling me? We're divorced."

"I just had a very ugly run in with Phil at the neighborhood luncheon," she said. "He was very rude. He said he knew what I had done and it was a shame I was still in the neighborhood."

"And what would you like me to do about it? Don't you have a fiancé you should be sending after him?"

"I'm disappointed in you," she said with disgust.

"That's too bad," I said dryly. "What will I do? Oh no, will you divorce me again?"

"This isn't funny," she said with a sigh. "We have to live here and see these people every day."

I blew out a breath. "Let me see if I can make this very clear. You are not a part of my life and vice versa. I don't know why you feel you can or should call me all the time, but you need to stop. This is all over. I don't want to go to such great lengths to block your number, but I will. I need a clean break. You did what you did. Own it. I'm moving on with my life. Happy trails to you and Phil, good luck with the neighbors and please, for the love of anything holy, don't call me again."

I ended the call and shut the thing off. That sealed it. I was leaving early. I would sit on the dock all damn day if I had to. I just had to get away. I didn't care if it made me a coward, but I wanted to run away from all of it.

When I arrived at the coast, I checked the time. I was going to be early, but I didn't mind the wait. I climbed out of the cab and grabbed my suitcase and sleeping bag. I was ready to be on that island. Hell, I would swim myself if there was a chance I'd make it out to the island. I took my stuff to the bench facing the water and had a seat. It was a nice view. I was strongly considering moving out to the coast. I could afford a second home. Maybe I would do it. Hell, maybe I would buy one of the many islands that were just off the coastline.

We'd see how this little adventure went. My ride should be showing up pretty quickly. I tapped my foot and waited. I had brought along the bottle of scotch to finish. Last night, it had felt wrong to be imbibing such a fine scotch while inside. I wanted to drink it while I was on the beach under the stars.

I spaced out a bit while I watched the water ebb and flow. It wasn't long before I heard the engine of a boat. An old man pulled up to the dock and was climbing out of the boat when I whistled to get his attention.

"What can I do for you?" he asked as he hobbled along the dock.

"I think you're my ride," I said with a friendly smile.

"Your ride?" he asked. "Where you going?"

"I'm supposed to be heading out to an island," I told him. "Bar Island, if I remember correctly."

He scowled and rubbed a hand over his beard. "You sure about that?"

"Pretty sure," I said. "Is that not the name of it? It's got a single house on the island. Privately owned. A rental." I waited for him to show some kind of recognition.

"Oh, I recognize it all right," he said. "I just came back from there."

"Oh?" I asked. "Are you the caretaker?"

"Nah, not really," he shrugged. "I help out the owner's kids. Technically, I guess they are the owners of it now. They don't much care to be out there. In order to pay the taxes, they rent it out. I knew their old man; he lived out there full time. I help them out because I don't want them to sell it. Their daddy would just hate the idea of it being taken out of the family."

I nodded. I didn't really care, but I listened. "I reserved it for the month," I told him.

He scowled and rubbed the beard again. "You and the missus?"

"Missus?"

"The pretty blonde I just took out there," he said. "Is that your lady? You lucky man."

Considering Amanda had brown hair, I knew it wasn't her. "I don't have a missus," I told him. "Maybe we're talking about a different island."

He smirked and shook his head. "I only go to one."

"I have the reservation," I said.

He shrugged. "She beat you to it."

"That can't be," I said. "I already paid."

"I think there's been a mistake," he said. "I don't have anything to do with the reservations. I just pick up groceries and make sure the place isn't being squatted in."

"I'd like to go out," I said. I wasn't going to give up. I had been waiting for this vacation for too long.

"You sure about that?" he asked.

"Yes," I nodded. "I can pay whoever is out there money to leave. I'm not giving up my reservation."

"Suit yourself," he said.

I grabbed my bag and sleeping bag and tossed it in the boat. "Just one woman?" I asked.

"Yes, sir," he said, and before he started the engine, he looked at me. "You're not a bad guy, are you?"

"Would a bad guy answer that with a yes?" I laughed.

"Don't need to," he said with another nod. "I know a good man when I see it. I find myself to be a very good judge of character. I have to make sure I'm looking out for the young lady."

"Young lady?" I asked with mild interest.

"Yep. What do you plan on telling her?"

"I plan on telling her there's been a mistake and she needs to leave," I said.

He laughed again and started the engine. "Oh, I'm sure that'll go over really well. Any woman willing to stay out there by herself for a month seems like she might be just a little stubborn."

"I can be just as stubborn," I said. "If she doesn't want to leave, that's okay. We'll share. I plan on sleeping under the stars anyway. I'm going to fish and be a beach bum. I need nothing else."

"Now, that's something I can relate to," he said.

I was hoping this stubborn, beautiful blonde he described would be reasonable. I wasn't going to give up and walk away. I needed this island retreat. I was certain I would suffocate if I didn't get this time away.

Mostly because I'd been planning on it for so long. If the woman wanted to get technical, we'd play the game of who saw it first. I was almost certain it was me. I had booked the cottage three months ago. It had been wide open.

"Is it pretty good fishing?" I asked him.

"Yep, if you know how to catch them," he laughed.

"I'm not worried about that," I said. "I've got a month to figure it out."

"If she lets you stay."

"If I let her stay," I corrected.

"Should I wait?" he asked as he approached the wooden dock that had seen better days.

"Nah, I'll let her have the house for a week if she wants it. I'll stay on the beach. If she doesn't want to share, I'll tell her to use the flare and signal you to come pick her up."

His choking laugh made me smile. "I think I might pay to see this little showdown."

"Nah, I'm a very reasonable man and I'm certain I can convince her it would be best if she gives me what I want," I said.

He offered to help me out of the boat, but I quickly declined. "Are you sure you don't want me to stick around?" he asked.

"I'll be fine," I told him. "She won't even know I'm here if that's what she wants. I'm a very quiet, private person."

"Just follow that path up to the house," he said. "Good luck. I think you might need it."

"Thanks," I said. "What was your name?"

"Captain Oleg Macdonald," he said proudly. "Holler if you need me." Then he burst into laughter. "Loudly."

"Will do," I said and waved. I headed up the path and inhaled. The first thing I smelled was the salty air. Then it was the damp foliage. Most of all, I smelled freedom. I took my time as I made my way up to the house. The front door was open.

I knocked on the door frame. "Hello?" I called out. "Anyone home?"

It seemed kind of silly to ask if anyone was home considering it was an island and she couldn't have gone far. I walked inside and looked around. There was a pile of clothing on the floor in the living room. That seemed a little odd. "Hello?" I called out again.

I popped into the bedroom and saw a bag on the bed. She must be out walking the island. I didn't dare intrude—yet. It did feel like she had claimed the cottage. I felt like I was breaking in, so I left my bag and suitcase on the porch and went to search for the mystery woman.

"Hello?" I called out as I walked through the trees.

I emerged from the trees and scanned the beach. I could see something not too far away, but I wasn't entirely sure what it was. It looked like a body. I was going to be so pissed if there was a dead body on my beach. The last thing I wanted was to deal with a crime scene. I would surely be pushed off the island. My entire vacation would be ruined.

"Please don't be dead," I whispered. "Hello?"

The body moved. "Thank goodness."

I waved my hand. "Hey!" I started walking towards the person. I assumed it was the woman Oleg had told me about.

The body sat up, then stood. "Holy shit," I breathed when I realized she was naked. Very naked. Nude. "Ho-ly shit."

I waved again. "Hello!"

She screamed and reached for the towel she'd been lying on. She haphazardly covered herself. That's when I realized I was scaring the shit out of her. I was a strange man on a private island she thought she had to herself. She was right to be terrified. I wasn't making the best first impression.

Chapter Five

Gabby

There was a man on my beach. My beach! I was naked as hell and he was standing fifteen feet away from me. This was bad. This was unacceptable. I stared at the man who looked like he'd been kissed by an angel or one of those Greek gods. He had to be a good six-three, maybe six-four. He had an athlete's body. The black hair cut short actually shone in the sunlight. He was wearing sunglasses, blocking his eyes, but I knew he was looking at me.

"Turn around!" I shrieked.

He laughed and put a hand over his eyes before giving me his back. "Sorry," he said. "I wasn't expecting to find you naked."

"Why were you expecting to find me at all?" I snapped. I secured the towel around me just a little better. Unfortunately, it wasn't a very big towel. It barely covered my bits.

"That's something we need to talk about," he said without looking back at me.

"You need to get off my island," I barked. "It's an island! You can't just come walking up!"

"I wasn't aware you owned the island," he chuckled.

"How did you get here?"

"Our good friend, Captain Oleg."

I was having a conversation with a stranger while standing nude in the middle of the day on what I thought was a private beach. Of all the things I thought I was going to do this month, this was not one of them.

"I would suggest you go get right back on that boat with Captain Oleg," I said calmly. "I will call the authorities."

I knew how ridiculous that sounded, but it just came out. I was hoping to scare the man away. He took a quick look over his shoulder at me and flashed me a thousand-watt grin that would probably disarm most women. In fact, I was sure most women would have eagerly dropped the towel and welcomed a man like him into their arms.

He turned back around. "If you'd like to grab the flare, go ahead. I'll wait."

He was being sarcastic. The man was actually cracking jokes while I was having one of those nightmares. The kind of nightmare we all had at some point in our lives. You find yourself at a party with colleagues only to find out you're naked. Or you're giving a speech and you're standing at the podium in your birthday suit.

"Sir, please, I don't know why you are here, but I need you to leave," I said calmly. I wasn't about to give in to hysteria. "I think there's been a mistake. Maybe this is a joke. Whatever the case may be, I would like you to leave now."

"I don't think that's going to happen," he laughed. "I'm an okay swimmer, but there's no way I can haul my ass ten miles back to the mainland."

The blood rushed from my face. "What?"

"I'm pretty sure the boat is gone," he said again.

"Didn't he tell you I was here?" I shrieked. The real panic was bubbling up. "You can't be here."

"I understand this is a surprise," he said calmly. "Can we talk for a minute?"

"Talk! You want to talk? I'm naked!"

"Yes, yes you are," he said. "I'll wait while you get dressed."

"I don't want to get dressed," I complained.

He stole another look over his shoulder. The damn dark glasses kept me from seeing what he was really thinking. "Suit yourself."

It looked like he was going to turn around again. “Don’t you dare! I’m going to the cottage to get dressed. You stay right here.”

“I’ll do that,” he said with a small laugh.

To walk away meant flashing him my backside. Lowering it meant exposing my breasts. This was not how this day was supposed to go. “Don’t you dare watch me,” I warned him.

“I’m a gentleman,” he said. I could hear the laughter in his voice. I was not happy. This was not funny.

I carefully walked sideways with a death grip on the towel. I made it into the tree line, which offered me some slight cover and stomped up the path to the cottage. A suitcase and a rolled up sleeping bag were sitting on the porch. Clearly, the man thought he was going to stay. I stomped inside and kicked the door closed behind me.

I snatched up my clothes and carried them into the bedroom to dress. “This is such crap,” I hissed.

I jerked on my clothes. I didn’t even know who I was supposed to be mad at. Oleg? The man knew damn well I was here. Why would he bring out a stranger? The stranger standing on the beach seemed like a good place to direct my anger, but was it really his fault? Ultimately, it had to be the owners of this cottage. Once again, I wondered if it was a scam. It had all seemed too good to be true and now I suspected it was. This was the kind of thing I’d read about. Some scammer got their hands on property information and rented it out with zero care about the people who were supposed to be staying at the place.

“How many more people are going to show up?” I muttered.

Dreams of naked days on the beach evaporated. I had no idea what I was going to do. I felt overwhelmed. I had put so much stock into this vacation. To think of it blowing up in my face was unfathomable. I needed to pull it together. I had to calm down and be rational. I was an ED doc. I dealt with insurmountable pressure every single day. This was not the end of the world.

I buttoned my shorts and used my fingers to comb through my hair. I wasn't expecting company and knew I probably looked a little rough. Not that it mattered. This was not supposed to be a hookup. I was supposed to be alone.

"Hello?" I heard the man call out.

I rolled my eyes. The downside of an island. There was nowhere to run. I was stuck with this character. I couldn't hide. I could try, but it wasn't like he wouldn't find me. I needed to feel him out. Was he dangerous?

Dangerously handsome.

I jerked open the bedroom door to find him standing in the now open front door. "Why'd you do that?" I asked.

"Do what?"

"You opened the door! Do you always knock after you've opened someone's door?"

"No," he said with a shrug.

He pushed up his sunglasses and I was hit with the most gorgeous, deep blue eyes I'd ever seen. The black lashes and thick black brows made them look even bluer. He had a dark tan, like he spent his days outside. The tanned skin made his perfect teeth look even whiter. The guy looked like he might be an underwear model. I quickly scanned his body and declared him fit and healthy. Probably about two-ten, two-twenty with very little body fat. I gave myself a mental shake. He wasn't a patient. I wasn't sizing him up to dose him with meds.

"Why are you still here?" I snapped.

"Because we're on an island and I don't have a boat," he answered matter-of-factly. "I already told you I'm not a great swimmer."

I scoffed and looked at the muscular arms visible with the tank top he was wearing. "I doubt that."

He offered a crooked smile. "I think we might have gotten off on the wrong foot," he said and extended his hand. "I'm Jake, Jake Wolfe."

I looked at his hand and then back into his eyes. I gave him a weak shake. "I don't care."

"I'm sorry for crashing your party," he said easily. "I didn't mean to sneak up on you."

"While I was naked," I added. "Naked. On the beach. I thought I was alone."

"I'm sorry about that," he said and looked properly remorseful. "I didn't know I'd find you in that position."

"You shouldn't have found me at all," I shot back. "I don't understand why you are here. This is a private island."

"I think we might have been double booked," he said.

I stared at him for several seconds. "What?"

"I paid for this property," he said. "I rented it for the next month."

I couldn't believe what I was hearing. "No," I breathed.

He nodded. "Yes."

I didn't know how to react. I had no words. So, I did the only thing I could think to do. I shut the door in the man's face. I had to. I couldn't keep looking at him. It felt like trying to look at the sun. He was so attractive. Too attractive. I couldn't think straight with those blue eyes were staring at me. Seriously blue. Like cobalt blue. It had to be colored contacts. There was no way anyone had those eyes naturally.

I shook my head and forced myself to pull it together. His eyes were not the most important topic at hand. I had much bigger problems I needed to deal with.

Chapter Six

Jake

I stared at the blue door and replayed the last fifteen minutes. The good news was she wasn't an old woman. The bad news was she didn't like me on sight. That made sense, given the way we met. I still didn't know her name, but I knew what she looked like naked. I'd been out of the dating game a while, but I was certain the rules were still the same. You met a person, got their name, and if there was a stroke of luck, you saw them naked.

We'd missed a few steps. Although, it did remove any mystery. If I would have seen her with her clothes on, I would have done my best to imagine what she looked like without them on. It was probably a total dick thing to do, but I was a man. A man who had been celibate for just a little too long. Seeing a beautiful woman lying naked on a beach was bound to stir up some images.

Setting aside the naked woman, there was an actual problem that needed to be solved. It wasn't going to do any good staring at a door. I knocked on the door once and waited. "Hello?" I called out. "We need to talk about this."

She didn't open it. I really didn't want to come off as aggressive, but I did pay for the place. When it came right down to it, this island was as much mine as it was hers. I knocked again. "I'm sorry to be a pain in the ass, but we need to figure this out."

The door jerked open. Her green eyes flashed at me. I wasn't sure why she was pissed at me. I sure as hell didn't do anything wrong. With the way she was looking at me, I expected her to start cursing at me. She was obviously pissed. Then, to my surprise, she closed the door again.

Now it was my turn to get pissed. This was going nowhere fast. I raised my hand to knock again when she opened the door once again. She looked calm, which was just a little scary considering she looked like she was ready to rip my head off a few seconds ago. I never considered the idea I might have just put myself on an island with an unstable woman. I'd seen enough documentaries to know it wasn't just guys who could fly into a murderous rage. This really might not have been my smartest move.

"What do you mean you booked this place for a month?" she asked calmly.

"I paid to rent the cottage and the island for the entire month of June," I said.

I could see the wheels turning behind those eyes that seemed to flare and retreat with her mood. "I believe there's been a mistake."

Finally, a sense of reason. "Yes, I believe so. Can we start over?"

"Start over?" she repeated.

"Yes, we kind of got off on the wrong foot," I laughed.

"You mean because you walked up and caught me naked on the beach?" she said with a forced smile.

She was a beautiful woman. Pouty lips, high cheekbones, and no make-up. There were freckles across her nose giving her a youthful appearance. I pegged her to be late twenties. She was a woman who took care of herself. She wasn't skinny but had the body of someone who either ran or did a lot of yoga.

I grinned and had the good sense to look sheepish. I shoved my hands in the pockets of my cargo shorts and looked down at my feet. "Yeah, something like that." I looked up and once again, redid my introduction. "Like I said, my name is Jake Wolfe. I'm not a crazy ax murderer or other type of violent criminal. Your body, fine as it is, is safe from me."

That seemed to relax her a bit. "I'm Gabby," she said. "Gabriela Kingston, but Gabby works."

"It's nice to meet you," I said, and shook her hand again. "Should we sit down?"

I didn't want to invade her space, and gestured to the rocking chairs on the covered porch. She stepped out and sat down in one while I sat down in the other. "Did you really rent this place?" she asked.

"Yes," I answered. "I didn't bring my receipt, but the fact I'm here kind of says I knew about it. Would I come all the way out here if I didn't have a reservation?"

"Is there a chance you got the dates wrong?" she asked.

"Uh, no," I shook my head. "I booked this place almost three months ago. What about you?"

She cringed, and I knew I had beat her to the punch on that front. "Not that long ago," she said. "Just a few weeks ago."

"So, we both reserved the place," I said with a nod. "Not trying to be creepy, but are you alone out here?"

"That is a little creepy," she said with a small laugh.

"Sorry."

"Yes, alone. You?"

I nodded once. "Yep."

"I hate to say it, but I was here first," she said.

I had to laugh at the very childish sentiment. "I reserved it first."

"But I was here first," she said. "Where did you come from?"

"A boat?"

"I mean, how far did you travel?" she asked.

There was a good chance I was going to lose this round. "Not far."

"How far?" she asked again.

"I live about an hour inland," I said.

"Ha! I live in LA. I traveled eight hours to get here."

"But I booked first," I shot back.

She rolled her eyes at me. "I can't just take a month off again."

"What do you do?" I asked. I had a feeling I was going to lose this round as well, considering I didn't have a typical nine to five job. I didn't have kids or pets to plan a trip around. Hell, I didn't even have plants to worry about.

She hesitated before answering. "I'm a doctor."

That was a surprise. "A doctor?"

"You act like that's a shock," she said.

"You're young," I blurted out.

"Not that young," she replied. "I'm an emergency room doctor. I've banked this vacation time for two years. It took a lot of work to get my schedule cleared for a month."

I was definitely going to lose this round. "I see."

"You?" she asked.

"Me?" I murmured in an attempt to stall.

"What do you do?"

"I own a company," I said.

"Oh. I suppose you had to jump through hoops as well."

I could have agreed with her, but I didn't want to lie. "Not exactly. I own the company. I no longer manage it. I do, but I don't. I have a COO that manages the day to day."

She crossed her arms over her chest. "Then I think it's settled."

"What's settled?" I asked.

"I get to stay, and you can come back when I leave at the end of the month," she stated like the matter had been resolved.

"I don't think it's settled at all," I said. "I'm here. Despite not going into the office every day, I did have to move some things around to be here. I've been planning this vacation for months. I *need* this vacation."

"As do I," she said.

I stared out at the water barely visible through the trees. There was no way I could walk away from all of this. "I can't leave," I said quietly.

"Well, I'm sorry, but I'm here. I've already settled in. I don't have a flight out. You live here. You can just go home."

"I don't want to," I said firmly. "Look, I rented the cottage, but I never intended to actually stay in it. You can have the cottage. I'll sleep on the beach. I would like to use the shower now and then, but I plan on fishing most of the time. Speaking of, I paid for groceries. Are they here?"

She wrinkled her nose. "That explains the salami," she muttered.

"So, my grocery order was filled," I said and took the small win. "Did you order groceries?"

"Yes, and they are here."

"We both want this vacation," I said. "The island is big enough for us to split in two. You take the west side and I'll take the east side. You can be naked as you want, and I'll mind my business on the other side. I won't see you. You won't see me. We'll work out a showering schedule. I might need to access my groceries on occasion, but we can work that out as well."

"No."

I raised an eyebrow. "You're pretty good at negotiating," I said dryly.

"I'm not going to share a house with a total stranger," she said.

"I'm not trying to share the house with you," I retorted. It was beginning to feel like a conversation with my ex-wife. She was being completely unreasonable and irrational.

"The island, whatever," she waved her hand. "I specifically chose this place because I want to be alone. All alone."

"Lady, I'm not trying to be your best friend," I snapped. "I want to be alone as well. Trust me, the last thing I wanted was to spend a month with a woman."

"Then leave," she shot back.

"You leave!"

"No way," she shook her head.

Tempers were not going to get us anywhere. I took a deep breath and remembered the old saying about catching more flies with honey than vinegar. "Look, we're both disappointed our dream vacation has been thwarted. That doesn't mean we have to let the mistake ruin our vacations. I'm willing to compromise. I've already said you can have the bed. I'll sleep outside."

"And when it rains?" she asked. "Am I supposed to sleep in the same house as you? I don't know you."

"No, you don't," I replied. "I don't want to know you. I don't want to hang out with you. I want to hang out on the beach. Nothing personal, but I didn't come here to make friends."

"Neither did I," she shot back.

"Look, this could be good for you," I said and tried another tactic. "You could get hurt or some random fishermen or boaters could dock. You're a young woman out here alone."

She gave me a dry look. "I'm not helpless. I live in LA. I have to deal with violent gang bangers, drunk and abusive men, and mentally ill patients on a daily basis. I can handle myself."

I couldn't seem to win with her. "Okay, then you being around might be good for me. I tend to do stupid shit. You can save me."

I waited and hoped she would see I was being reasonable. I felt like I was the one making the bulk of the compromise. I was giving up the cottage. She was being completely unreasonable and stubborn. If she could just try and see my side of things, we might be able to come to some kind of resolution. She seemed like a reasonable person, but I was beginning to think otherwise.

"I can't do it," she said. "I don't know you. I don't care if you seem nice enough. I need to be alone."

"You'll be alone," I insisted. "You won't see me."

"I'm sorry, but I'm going to have to ask you to leave the island," she said. "I was here first and I'm not comfortable with you being here."

I could sit here and argue with her, or I could grab the flare and hope Oleg wasn't too far away. I had come out here to get away from people. From one particular woman. My mental health would not tolerate an entire month with someone who was not going to give an inch. I was expected to give up everything to please a woman. I couldn't do it.

"I'll try and catch Oleg," I said. "Where's the flare gun?"

"I don't know," she said, and got up to search for it.

I grabbed my suitcase and stuck my sleeping bad under my arm. I took one last look around and started down the path. I was hoping like hell Oleg was still at the dock. When I broke through the trees, there was nothing. I didn't even see a boat in the distance. Oleg was long gone. And I was stranded.

"I found it!" Gabby said as she jogged down to the dock.

"He's gone," I said. "Long gone. I told him we'd work something out."

"We'll shoot the flare," she said and shoved the gun at me.

"It's the middle of the day with his back to us," I said. "He's not going to see it."

She stared at me with her jaw hanging open. "What does that mean?"

"It means you're going to have to share your little island," I said. "Or I'm going to share. Depends on how you want to look at it."

"I didn't agree to this," she said with disgust.

"I didn't agree to sharing my reservation with you either," I reminded her. "You have no more claim to this place than I do. We both paid to stay here. We both bought groceries. You don't own the island any more than I do. I've offered a compromise."

"That's unacceptable."

"Write a letter," I shot back and started back up to the house.

Chapter Seven

Gabby

I watched him walk away. He was actually going to stay. This was a nightmare. I couldn't believe this was happening. I couldn't let it happen. I had to fight for my right to complete and total privacy. I started following him up the path.

"Where are you going?" I asked what had to be the dumbest question ever given we were on an island.

"I need to get a few things," he said without looking back at me.

"Like what?"

"Like some of the food I paid for," he said with obvious irritation.

He pushed open the front door and walked right into the kitchen. I watched in horror as he opened the fridge and helped himself to the contents. "What are you going to do?" I asked him.

"I'm getting some food and the stuff I need to build a fire on the beach," he answered.

"You can't be serious," I said.

He pointed to the sleeping bag he had deposited on the floor. "I'm very serious. I came here to sleep outside. I wasn't making that up."

"What if—" I stopped when I realized we were on an island and the chances of a bear sneaking up on him was pretty slim. Not impossible, but slim.

"What if what?" he asked and stuffed some stuff into his backpack. "I'm leaving my suitcase here. Please don't toss it outside."

"Why are you doing this?" I asked with disgust.

"Because I'm on vacation and I want to sleep on the beach," he said.

"You can't stay here," I said and stopped myself from stomping my foot.

"I'm not staying in here," he said and picked up the bag. "I'm staying out there. You stay in here and do whatever it was you were planning to do before I showed up. Your body is safe with me. I'm not touching you. I'm not bothering you. I'd ask you to do the same."

"For how long?" I asked.

"I have a feeling that Oleg might be back tomorrow," he said with a smirk.

"Why do you think that?"

"Because if he spent twenty minutes with you, he probably knows what I'm up against," he said.

He was insulting me. "Are you suggesting I'm difficult?"

"Not really a suggestion."

"I don't understand why he brought you here at all," I said again. "He knew I was out here."

"To be fair to Oleg, he did warn me," he said with a small laugh. "It's my own fault for ignoring the warning."

"Warning!" I gasped. "You're being very rude."

"You're not exactly being polite," he shot back without missing a beat.

"I'm not trying to be rude," I said and reminded myself to stay calm. "This was unexpected. It isn't every day I get stranded on an island with a strange man. I'm not sure what the social rules are."

"General politeness seems like a good place to start," he said. "I tried to be reasonable. I offered a compromise. You're the one who dug in and all but planted her flag on an island she doesn't own. I have just as much at stake here as you do. This was my vacation after a very long year. I'm not exactly keen to share it either, but I was willing to do it to keep the peace."

"I'm sorry if I was rude," I finally said. "I just really don't want to be here with you."

"Ditto," he said. "When Oleg comes back tomorrow, I'll go. I'll get a refund and reschedule my entire vacation to please you. Does that make you happy?"

Now I felt bad. "I wasn't trying to ruin your vacation."

"Then congratulations," he said with a tight smile. "You succeeded in doing something without even trying."

"Jake," I said and felt a sense of familiarity using his first name. It seemed to strike a chord in him as well.

"What?" he asked.

I nibbled my lower lip. "Do you really think Oleg will come back tomorrow?"

He looked disappointed by my question. "I don't know. If he doesn't, we'll figure it out then. I'll stay out of your way."

"I'm not trying to be rude," I said in defense of my actions. "I don't want to ruin your vacation, but this is important to me and I really don't know if I will ever get another chance to do this."

"Got it."

"Should you take something?" I asked.

"Like?"

"I don't know, a blanket? Maybe a pillow? I feel like I'm throwing you out in the cold."

"You are, but it's not cold and I want to be out," he said with another cocky smile. "Trust me, I think the accommodations will be much better."

He was angry with me and I couldn't really blame him. "Do you, uh, want to make a sandwich or something?"

"No."

"What are you going to eat?" I asked.

He tapped his backpack. "I've got a can of tuna and crackers. Tomorrow, I'll hopefully be able to catch some breakfast while I wait for Oleg to return."

"You're a large man," I said without realizing what I was saying until the words were out of my mouth. "I mean, tuna and crackers don't really seem like they'll be enough for you."

"I've got a bottle of scotch I've been saving for this very special first night," he said.

I immediately pulled back. I wasn't sure I liked the idea of him drinking a bottle of scotch while we were alone on an island. "I see."

"Trust me, Gabby, your body is safe from me," he said with a smile that disarmed all my defenses. "I have no intention of hooking up. I really, really just want to be alone. Me, the bottle of scotch, and my crackers are all I need. And my sleeping bag. Have a good night."

He walked past me without saying another word. I didn't like that he was mad at me. I shouldn't have cared, but by nature I was a people pleaser. I liked to make people happy. I was a doctor because I wanted to help people when they were at their worst. But this man didn't need me. He was obviously very self-reliant.

I closed the door behind him and locked it for good measure. I didn't want to risk him coming in while I was asleep. I was seriously hoping the grizzly captain would be back in the morning. I didn't think I could spend an entire week with him. That would be too weird. As bad as I felt for ruining his vacation, I had to take care of myself. He was some bigshot business owner. He could come back next month.

"Not my problem," I assured myself.

My plans for a long, late evening on the beach were ruined. The place did have an old-fashioned claw-foot tub that was very inviting. I was going to make myself something to eat and then take a nice, long soak in the tub.

My first instinct was to tell Alexa to play some music. I laughed aloud to myself. It was my first of what would probably be many reality checks. There was an old school record player on a shelf with some actual records below it. I wasn't even sure I knew how to use the damn thing, but I was going to try.

I sifted through the albums. There were a lot of classic rock albums and a few Elvis albums. My mother loved Elvis. I had grown up listening to him. I hadn't really come out here to get nostalgic, but this vacation was also supposed to be a time to heal. After losing both of my parents and never properly grieving, it was time. I didn't feel like crying necessarily, but I did feel like I owed them each a quiet moment.

I put the album on and smiled as the familiar sound filled the cottage. With a little background noise, I opened the fridge and started looking around for what I wanted to eat. I wasn't really hungry. The whole day was taking a toll. I grabbed the box of crackers and pulled the tray of sliced cheese from the fridge. It was time for another glass of wine.

"In the ghetto," I sang and swayed to the music while munching on my cheese and cracker dinner.

I told myself I was going to enjoy the quiet, but it was *really* quiet. After finishing my dinner, I started to run the bath water. There was a basket on a shelf filled with small bottles of bubble bath. I selected one with mint and dumped it in the tub. Tempted as I was to stroll through the cottage naked, I reminded myself I wasn't all that alone. There was no reason to give the man another peep show.

While in the bedroom, I caught a glimpse of movement outside the open window. Expecting to see a bird, I walked over to see what kind of wildlife I was going to be dwelling with during my time on the island.

"Oh shit," I gasped.

It was not a bird that I saw. It was Jake. He dropped a small log on the fire he'd built on the beach. I watched him squat beside it and blow. The flames rose and he smiled. My heart skipped a beat. He stood back up and unrolled his sleeping bag. I couldn't tear my eyes away. This was wrong. He wanted to be alone. I wanted to be alone. I had accused the man of being a creeper and I was the one creeping on him.

"Dammit," I whispered.

Why did I have to get stranded with the sexiest man on the planet? I watched him for a few more minutes. Much to my surprise, he reached behind him and pulled off his tank top. He was all tanned skin and muscles. The niggle of guilt in the back of my mind was quickly shut down. He'd seen me butt naked. It was only fair I got to catch a glimpse of him.

"Oh shit," I gasped when the man dropped the cargo shorts.

I should have looked away. It was impolite to stare. I was the peeping tom in this scenario. But part of me wanted to see if he was going to take it all off. As if he sensed me watching, he glanced over his shoulder. I dropped. I hit the floor below the window and burst into a fit of giggles. I was acting like a teenage girl caught spying.

He wanted one night alone on the island. I could give him that. I very carefully got back to my feet and peered over the windowsill. I didn't see him by the fire anymore. I squinted and he appeared out of the water like a magical merman. He threw his head back and swiped his hands over his face. He was braver than I. Although, I probably would have gotten into the water had he not shown up.

Was he naked? It was probably best I didn't know. I closed the blinds and pulled the ugly plaid curtains over them. I didn't want to be tempted to peep at the man while he slept. Knowing he was occupied, I was emboldened to strip naked. After refilling my wineglass, I headed into the bathroom and sank into the hot water.

Elvis was still crooning, and I finally felt at peace. It was a little disconcerting to know there was a man maybe seventy feet away. Possibly naked and very hot. That didn't matter. This was not that kind of a vacation. Although, I was supposed to be on vacation to blow off a little stress. A torrid love affair on a deserted island was the stuff written about in the novels I considered to be my guilty pleasure.

I couldn't stop wondering what he was doing out there. Was he naked and sitting by the fire? Was he naked and eating his tuna and crackers? There was a theme to my line of thinking. Naked. Tomorrow, he had to go. I didn't think I trusted myself to be alone with him. Not that he was the least bit interested in me. I had been pretty rude and maybe just a little obnoxious. I was positive I was not on his good side. He didn't like me.

The chances of him being attracted enough to have sex with me was slim to none. That was fine. I wasn't here to get laid. I was unwinding. I was getting centered and all that other stuff. No funny business.

But he was just beyond my window. It was like holding out a piece of candy and telling a child he couldn't have it. A little peeking wouldn't hurt anyone.

Chapter Eight

Jake

I stood up, water sluicing down my chest. Damn, it felt good to be in the water. It felt so freeing. There was something about being weightless. I ran my hands over my face before pushing the water from my hair. The fire on the beach was dying and needed some attention. I had only meant to take a quick dip, but once I got in the water, I couldn't bring myself to get out.

I walked through the water with my toes digging into the sandy bottom. My underwear clung to my skin. I didn't hesitate to strip out of them and walk in the nude the rest of the way. The last thing I needed was to chafe. Besides, my backpack had a change of clothes. After putting a log on the fire, I stood in front of it to dry off.

I understood why she'd been naked on the beach. There was something about being in the flesh under what was now a half-moon in the sky that was very freeing. It made a guy feel alive. It was the most alive I had felt in a good ten years. If I was being honest with myself, which was something I had been doing a lot of lately, I hadn't been happy in my marriage for a long time. We were two very different people. There was no overlap in our interests, and neither of us seemed to care enough about the other to try and find common ground.

I reached into my bag and pulled out a clean pair of boxer briefs. I wasn't going to bother getting dressed up for a night alone on the beach. I sat down on the sleeping bag and pulled out the can of tuna. I had hoped to be dining on fish tonight, but no use crying over spilled milk. I had argued my case and lost. Tomorrow, I was going home.

When I got home, I was going to call the owner of this little island and give them a piece of my mind.

As angry as I was, I wanted to come back. This was a piece of paradise I wasn't willing to give up. I didn't care if they gave me a break on the cost for the next month. I wanted to be here. I stared out at the water with the moonlight reflecting on the calm surface. I wanted to say I could live like this, but that probably wasn't true. It was nice right now, but I imagined it would get very old after a few months. There was something to be said for technology and convenience. I loved a good hamburger and the occasional trip to the theater.

I took a bite of my dinner and had to smile. This had been a staple back in the day. When I was a teenager, I would pack a backpack, hop in my truck, and drive up to the mountains for an overnight retreat. My parents were used to me disappearing. As long as I trained hard and didn't get into trouble, they pretty much let me do what I wanted.

I smiled at the memory of one of my nights in the woods. I had been sitting in front of a fire just like this, munching on my tuna and crackers when I saw a bear. The damn thing hadn't been too far away. It watched me watch it. It was the tuna. In my young, teenage mind, I never considered the idea I wasn't the only one in the woods dining on fish.

That memory drifted right into a memory of Amanda. I hated that she still haunted my thoughts. It pissed me off that she still took up so much damn real estate in my head. I knew it was going to take a while to completely exorcise her from my brain. I'd been with her nearly half my life. That wasn't something that just went away after signing my name on divorce papers.

I didn't miss her. I knew I didn't love her. It was an absence. At one of my meetings with my attorney, he recommended I seek grief counseling. I thought the man had lost his damn mind. He said he referred all his clients because it helped with the divorce process. It cooled the anger that was generally a result of the pain of a divorce. I didn't go to a therapist, but I did do a little reading and I discovered I was grieving.

I grieved the loss of a dream. I grieved the loss of the life I thought I had. For me, the death of our marriage had been dragging on for years. I was too much of a sucker to walk out on her. I kept thinking I could fix what was broken between us.

And then there was the tuna and crackers. I stared at the sleeve of crackers in my hand and actually laughed. After a whole hell of a lot of cajoling and downright begging, I had convinced her to take a trip with me. We'd gone to a very romantic cabin in the woods. We were sitting around the firepit – propane, not actual fire – and I had busted out my favorite campfire snack.

The woman actually gagged and cringed at the idea of dipping a Saltine into a can of cold tuna. Amanda had been raised very differently than I. She didn't appreciate some of the most basic pleasures in life, like tuna fish. She didn't mind grilled tuna steaks, but heaving forbid anything that came from a can. It wasn't until we'd been married a couple of years that I actually got to go to her family home.

Amanda was a fraud. She'd grown up in a trailer park. Her parents were in and out of jail. She traded on her looks, and had become very skilled at spotting the men with money. Vulnerable men, as far as I was concerned. Somehow, the woman saw something in me. She hooked her wagon to me, and I was stupid enough to believe she did it because she loved me. Looking back, I realized she'd been managing me. We met because she was my financial advisor. She advised me right into making a fortune and reaped the benefits. I supposed that's why I didn't hate the idea of giving her half of everything. My success had been the result of her pushing. She knew who to schmooze to get the investment capital. She'd smiled and flirted with the people that helped my business get off the ground.

I reached for the backpack and pulled out the scotch. I held it in my hands and stared at the label in the firelight before looking up at the millions of stars overhead. "Goodbye, Amanda."

I wanted the scotch, but this didn't feel quite right. There was an angry woman not too far away. The scotch was supposed to be a celebration of my freedom. I didn't feel entirely free just yet. I couldn't completely relax. I was still an intruder. Amanda had made me feel like the intruder in my own house for a long time. The weight of our broken marriage had been hanging on me for years. Tonight was supposed to the first night I was free.

I wasn't free. I couldn't howl at the moon after I had a few. That would only serve to bring my roommate running and screaming at me to keep it down. Although, if we were being fair, she wasn't exactly being quiet up there in the cottage. When I came out of the water, I heard the unmistakable sound of Elvis. I couldn't say that would have been my first choice in music, but as long as she was enjoying herself, so be it.

Tonight wasn't the night. I slid the bottle back into the backpack and reached for one of the bottles of water I had carried down with me. I turned to look up at the cottage. There was a soft glow coming from one of the windows. I wondered what she was doing up there all alone. I smiled at the memory of her naked on the beach. The look on her face had been priceless. It was too bad she hated me on sight. I kind of liked her. There was something different about her. I could honestly say I knew no woman who would be willing to come out here and stay all by herself. I worked with athletic women who did downhill skiing for fun. Women who loved white water rafting and climbing sheer rock cliffs. None of those women would be brave enough to come out here and stay by themselves for a month.

That alone made me want to get to know her. We clearly had at least one similar interest. It was just too bad she was so stubborn. Too bad she thought I was a pain in her ass, crashing her party. If she'd be just a little more open-minded, we might actually get along. We did seem to have a little in common. Maybe I would catch some fish in the morning and share with her.

That would be a real test. If I gifted Amanda some fresh, pan-fried fish, she would probably vomit. She liked fish, but not if she knew where it came from. If my lovely little Gabby ate the fish, she would forever hold a place in my heart. Not my actual heart, but she would be added to the very short list of women I respected and admired.

And then I would never see her again. I blew out a breath and shook my head. I was on a woman diet. I didn't trust my own judgement. The celibacy had helped me clear my head, and I did feel like I was in a better place, but I was still not ready to spar with a woman. It was going to be a while before I felt like I could get back into that game. I was much older, far more jaded, and just a little cynical.

I got to my feet and shook off the dark thoughts. I was out here to get Amanda out of my system. What happened, happened. It was time to start moving forward. "Shake it off," I muttered.

I was on a beautiful island for one night. I was not going to waste it by thinking about my ex-wife and lamenting the life I didn't get to have. I was going to focus on the life I did have and the life I planned on having. After walking off the negative that threatened to cast a pall over my one and only night, I climbed into my sleeping bag.

I stared up at the stars and quickly identified the Big Dipper. The stars were incredibly bright. The crickets were chirping all around me. The crackling of the fire mingled with the soft, gentle sounds of the water lapping against the shore. Even with the faint sound of Elvis in the background, the night was beautiful. It soothed me into a state of peacefulness I had not felt in a long time. Probably fifteen years. My soul had been craving this. I could practically feel my heart and soul knitting back together after being shattered. I was mending. I was healing. All it took was a night out under the stars. I was a little irritated with myself for not doing it earlier.

I closed my eyes and imagined a new world. I couldn't quite imagine my future yet because it was all a blank slate. I had money and didn't technically have to work. I could go anywhere and do anything. I just wasn't sure what it was I wanted to do. Would I ever really know?

Chapter Nine

Gabby

I thought I would be exhausted. Unfortunately, my mind and body was still on California time. Even though the clock told me it was midnight, it only felt like nine to me. I was used to running on four to five hours of sleep. I probably shouldn't have slept on the plane. While I was planning my vacation, I kept thinking about all the peace and quiet I was going to get. I didn't consider the idea the quiet might be too much. I was used to sleeping with my ceiling fan on. A fan in general. I was missing the noise. How was that even possible?

It was so damn quiet. There were no sirens or people talking. I almost missed my upstairs neighbors stomping around. Why weren't there any crickets? "My goodness," I complained and rolled to the side. "Only you could fly three-thousand miles to find quiet and then complain it was too quiet."

After another thirty minutes of tossing and turning, I got up and opened the bedroom window. I could hear the sound of the water, which I hoped was enough to create the white noise I needed to sleep. The sound was faint, but hopefully just enough to block out the weird buzzing noise I heard in the back of my mind. My dad used to tell me I had an internal motor that was constantly on the move. I was always thinking and planning, just like him. I used to think he was crazy, but I now understood what he was talking about.

It wasn't just the lack of white noise that was keeping me up. He was keeping me up. I couldn't get him out of my head. I wasn't normally the skittish type. I didn't walk down the city street and constantly look over my shoulder to see if the bogey man was chasing me. As part of my med school training, Dad had insisted I take self-defense classes. He said I would be dealing with unruly patients at times. He also worried about me being in the city by myself. I took the classes and did feel more confident after doing so. If my unwanted stranger tried anything funny, he'd be singing soprano for the rest of the month. I was a doctor and I knew exactly where to hit to make it hurt.

"Stop acting like you're a gladiator, Gabby," I scolded. I could talk a big talk, but when it came right down to it, I couldn't imagine actually hurting someone. That probably went against my Hippocratic Oath.

Of all the islands in the world, he lands on mine. And it was mine. I was firmly holding onto the idea that I was here first. I called dibs. He was probably some rich dude that could buy his own island if he wanted to. Having him out there was both oddly comforting and discomforting at the same time. I was independent and I felt like I could handle myself, but now that it was dark out, it was a little spooky. It was scarier here than being in a dark alley because at least in a dark alley, I could scream for help, I could call nine-one-one. Being utterly alone was appealing and scary at the same time. It was nice to know there was someone nearby. Assuming the someone wasn't the threat.

"Don't do it," I muttered. I was not going to go down the what if rabbit hole. I wasn't prone to anxiety, but like anyone else, I could have a wild imagination. It wouldn't take much effort to conjure up an ax murderer stalking me on a deserted island. I could already see the scenario unfolding in my mind. A boater would pull up to shore claiming to be out of gas or having engine trouble. I'd try to help only to discover the man was a creeper.

"Go to sleep," I groaned.

I was not a good sleeper. My mom used to tell me I was born that way. It took me forever to fall asleep. Unlike most kids, I functioned best on about six to seven hours. She always said I was born to be a doctor. That was great and all, but right now, I wanted to sleep. I tried everything and ended up tossing and turning into the wee hours of the morning. I was certain my unwanted guest would be gone when I finally dragged myself out of bed tomorrow. The encounter would be over, and I could get on with the rest of my vacation.

Alone. All alone.

My brain finally gave in and I could feel myself drifting off to sleep. It was a fitful sleep. Images of him floated through my dreams. I met hundreds of people a day and very few had the power to really stick with me. As a doctor, I was only able to function because I wore a Teflon skin. I couldn't absorb the grief. I couldn't get to know every patient and their family because it would tear me down. Most people thought me to be aloof, which I supposed I was. I had to be, for my own self-preservation.

Jake was proving to be dangerous. If he was already intruding into my subconscious mind, it meant he was in. I had a month to purge him from my thoughts. If I couldn't get rid of him, I was never going to get any real rest. I was here to shut down my brain and just chill.

I woke up and smelled coffee. That wasn't right. The cottage didn't have an automated pot. It was old and manual. In my semi-awake state, I wondered if it was drifting in from somewhere else. Then reality hit and I sat up. There was nowhere for the aroma of coffee to drift in from. The coffee had to be coming from inside the house, which meant *he* was inside the house!

I threw off the blankets and almost rushed into the living room when I remembered I was wearing nothing but a pair of panties and a tank top. I stopped, pulled on a pair of shorts and then rushed out to the living area. There he was. He wasn't gone. He was sitting at the old wooden table with a cup of coffee and a sandwich.

"Good morning," he said with a small wave. "Technically, I'm not sure it's morning anymore, but good day regardless."

I blinked and tried to put all the pieces together in my sleep-deprived brain. "What are you doing here?"

He picked up his sandwich. "Having lunch."

"Lunch?"

"It's almost noon and I've been up since dawn," he said with a shrug. "I'm hungry."

"But why are you here?" I asked again. "Like, in here. In *my* cottage."

I needed coffee. I walked to the pot and saw it was half full. I didn't care if he made it. I needed it. I found a mug and poured myself a cup. I took the first sip and waited for the caffeine to hit my bloodstream. It wasn't quite as strong as I was used to, but it would do. My sleep-deprived brain slowly came to life and putting together all the pieces.

I turned around to find him eating his sandwich like I wasn't even in the room. "So?" I asked.

"So, what?"

"Why are you here? I thought you said Oleg would be back in the morning."

"I hung out by the dock for a while and did some fishing. He never showed up and I didn't catch anything. I knocked on the door. No one answered. I assumed you were out walking or doing other things. I didn't think you would mind if I made myself a sandwich with *my* groceries."

"Other things?" I questioned.

"Yeah, like what you were doing yesterday," he said with a cocky grin. "I didn't dare intrude on that. I told you I would give you space. Go be naked. You do you."

"I'm not going to be sunbathing in the nude when you're here," I spat. My cheeks were burning, and it had nothing to do with the hot coffee pumping through my veins.

"I wasn't sure," he shrugged. "You have every right to do whatever it is that makes you happy. I'd probably do the same. In fact—"

"Don't say it," I muttered.

"What?"

"I know what you're going to say," I said.

"That I enjoyed a little al fresco myself last night," he laughed. "I see the appeal. Maybe once you go to your side, I might give the whole naked sunbathing thing a try. I just want to make sure you don't come traipsing along and catch me in my birthday suit."

"You cannot do that," I said aghast.

"Do what?"

"Be naked!" I shrieked.

"Didn't you say you were a doctor?" he asked, and took another bite of his sandwich.

I didn't understand how he was acting like this wasn't a big deal. This was horrifying. I couldn't stand here and talk to him about being naked. It was wrong. I wasn't that kind of girl. Was I?

"I am, but what does that have to do with anything?" I choked out.

"Aren't you used to seeing naked bodies? You've seen one, you've seen them all, right?"

He was teasing me. How dare he make light of this horrible situation?

"I would really prefer it if you just didn't."

"Didn't what?" he asked innocently.

"You know what," I said. "You're purposely trying to unnerve me."

"Not on purpose, but if that's what's happening, I do apologize."

He was still messing with me. "We should send up one of those flares," I suggested.

"I think that might be an abuse of the emergency alert system."

"This isn't funny," I said. "Seriously, we need to do something."

"*I* did do something," he said. "I slept on the beach. I was up at the crack of dawn waiting for a ride. I'll remind you again, I don't *have* to do shit. I have every right to be here. You might want to tone down the self-righteous indignation. I could very well change my attitude and insist you take your sweet little ass back to the mainland."

My mouth dropped open. He could certainly be assertive when he wanted to be. "I was here first."

He rolled his eyes. "Sticking with that line, are you?"

"Yes, I am."

"I reserved it first," he shot back. "As a matter of fact, why don't you pack your shit and go wait by the dock. I won't make you change the sheets before you go."

"Don't threaten me!"

"Not a threat, lady," he said without appearing to be the least bit upset. It was like he was used to dealing with these kinds of situations all the time. "I'm telling you to cool your jets. I'm being extremely reasonable but don't mistake my kindness for weakness. I've already said I will go, but I'm not about to put an old man out to suit your ridiculous demands. There's been a solution put on the table. I don't see you offering up any suggestions. You're just expecting me to bend to your whim. Like I said, I'm willing to give it up for a month. But this attitude you've got going isn't making me feel very generous."

I didn't particularly enjoy being threatened, and that's exactly what he was doing. Even if he was doing it with a smile on his face, I didn't like it. "I'm not expecting you to bend to my whim, but last night you agreed to go."

"I did, but we've also established I'm not about to swim. Just sit tight. If Oleg shows up, you bet your ass I'll be on that boat and out of here."

"That's the second time you've referenced my ass," I said.

He smirked and sipped his coffee. "Did you sleep well?"

I immediately put my hand to my hair. I was a restless sleeper. I gave the term bedhead new meaning. I was standing here in tiny shorts and a tinier tank with no bra and my hair a mess. That was just a little embarrassing.

"I slept fine," I snapped. "I'm going to shower. Maybe you should check and see if Oleg has come back."

"Do you really think he's going to come all the way out here, drive past the dock and head back?" he asked. "Doesn't it make more sense that he would maybe stop and see if we needed anything?"

I really hated how rational and logical he was. It made me feel like an idiot. "Well, we just don't know, do we?"

"I'm almost done eating," he said. I'll check in a bit. Or you could."

"This isn't going to work," I blurted out.

"What isn't going to work?"

"This," I gestured frantically to him at the table. "You sitting here eating lunch in my kitchen."

He held up a finger and slowly waggled it. "Careful there, you're heading back into the indignation territory. We've already established this is currently my kitchen as well. Don't get selfish."

"I'm not, but you said—"

"You're used to getting your way a lot, aren't you?" he asked.

"No, but—"

"Yeah, you are. Let me guess, you're not married."

I frowned at him. "What's that got to do with anything?"

He nonchalantly shrugged. "You live alone?"

"That's none of your business."

"So yes to both," he said with a laugh. "You're not used to compromise. Let me go a step further. You're an only child. You've never had to share your toys or your parents with siblings. You've clearly never had to share a room with anyone."

It was a little disturbing that he knew so much about me with me telling him nothing. "I'm going to shower," I said and spun on my heel.

I could hear him laughing as I walked back into the room. He really had no buttons to push. I, on the other hand, was all buttons. He was pushing them left and right. I needed to put on that thick skin I was so famous for. I only had to tolerate him for a little longer. If I wasn't nice, he would put up a fight. I didn't want that.

There was no lock on the bedroom door, which was unfortunate. I grabbed my fresh clothes and carried them across the hall to the bathroom. Thankfully, that door had a lock. I was used to locker rooms and all that, but this was a very different situation. None of the residents, nurses, or fellow doctors I worked with looked like him. None of them made me feel the way he did.

The lock saved me from doing something stupid, like inviting him into the shower with me. When I looked at myself in the mirror, I groaned.

"Lovely," I muttered.

As I suspected, my hair was matted and sticking up one side. The tiny bit of mascara I'd worn yesterday was smudged under my eyes. I looked rough. Here I was worried about him accosting me, but I was pretty sure a man like that would have no desire to jump my bones. I had no need to fear he was going to attempt to seduce me.

"Bummer," I muttered, and stripped before stepping into the shower. Oddly enough, I was regretting my decision not to pack more makeup. I pushed aside the thought. It didn't matter what I looked like. He was going to be gone and I was going to be all alone. Completely, utterly alone with the silence.

Chapter Ten

Jake

I got up and couldn't stop smiling. Sparring with my unwilling roommate was a lot more fun than sparring with Amanda. Seeing her wild hair and bare face was refreshing. I liked being able to wipe away that haughty exterior she seemed to wear all the time. I truly didn't know she was in bed when I let myself in. It was late in the day. I assumed she would be out on the beach or exploring the little piece of paradise we were sharing—for the moment.

I washed my plate and mug and figured I would wash hers as well. I needed a little goodwill with her. I was assuming, maybe hoping, Oleg would come back today. I didn't think he would really just leave the both of us out here. Yesterday, he probably thought it was funny to teach me a lesson. I got it. She was not a welcoming figure and wanted me off the island. Staying would only make it miserable for the both of us. It was best to wave the white flag and cut my losses. I would come back later or find another island to retreat to.

After cleaning up the nominal mess I had made, I went back outside to sit on the porch. If a boat came our way, I would hear it. And I was certain Oleg would come up to the cottage if he did show up. But what if he didn't show? That could end badly for me. She would make my life miserable if I was stuck here for a week. I didn't want to waste a month of vacation with this woman. She wanted me to be miserable. I could get that at home.

My only hope was that he would be out later today. Maybe he had stuff to do in the morning and would make it an afternoon run, like yesterday. The man had tried to warn me about Gabby, but I was too stubborn to listen. I should have known better. I was raised to respect my elders. He had more wisdom in his little finger than I had in my thirty-five years on the planet. I had been so dead set on getting my ass on this island, I didn't stop to think it might not be the best thing.

I took a long drink from the bottle of water and gently rocked back and forth in the rocking chair. It was a humid day, and I already slathered my skin with bug spray. Last night had taught me a hard lesson about who the king species on the island was. I was low on the food chain. The sky had been a pretty pink this morning, which told me there was a good chance we were in for a storm. I didn't see any dark clouds in the sky right now, but I'd spent enough time in the mountains to know weather could change in a flash.

I had left the front door open when I came out. The cottage was stuffy and needed a little fresh air. Not that it mattered to me, but it seemed like the right thing to do. She stood in the doorway, her hair wet and hanging around her shoulders. The look on her face spoke volumes. She was not happy. I was very familiar with the look of an unhappy woman, especially when I was the source of the unhappiness.

"You're still here," she said with a sigh.

"Appear to be." I nodded and turned my attention to the view once again. I loved a little sarcasm. More experience told me that was the exact way to piss off a woman. In this case, piss the woman off even more than she already was.

"Are you packed?" she asked with her hands on her hips like she was a mother scolding a naughty boy. The look irritated me. "Did you put out the fire?"

"Yes, Gabby," I said dryly. "I would never dare to leave a fire burning on your beach. I packed all my toys and remembered my toothbrush."

"I was just checking," she said with her chin raised.

"It's handled," I told her. "Believe it or not, I'm a very capable adult who can handle his shit."

She stood in the doorway for several minutes. I assumed she was expecting me to say something about leaving. I had nothing to say. Maybe she was hoping to stare me into walking away. The woman didn't know who she was messing with. I could stare down an opponent with the best of them. I wasn't about to tuck tail and run.

"I'm going to go for a walk," she announced as if she was expecting me to roll out the red carpet for her.

"Good," I said. "You should. It's beautiful out there."

She didn't walk away. "Well, I guess if Oleg comes while I'm gone, it was nice to meet you. Good luck, and all that."

I had to laugh. "Was it?"

"Was it what?" she asked with a cute little scowl.

"Nice to meet me?" I grinned. "I get the feeling you're just saying that. I hope you don't expect me to say it back."

"Okay, it wasn't nice, but that's what people say," she lectured. "Despite your total lack of manners, I do hope you get a chance to come back. I would hate to think I ruined your vacation."

"Me too," I said. "You did."

"Goodbye," she said and stepped off the porch.

"It was nice to meet you Gabby," I said with total seriousness. "Even if we didn't get off on the right foot. I hope you enjoy your vacation, and you find whatever it is you are looking for."

"Thanks," she murmured.

I watched her walk away. It was a damn shame we were like oil and water. We did share some of the same interests. If she could just set aside her nasty stubbornness and the idea she was entitled to something I felt we were both entitled to, we could be friends. Maybe a little something more. A fling on vacation was just what the doctor ordered. Or not. It was probably best I didn't get entangled with someone. I didn't need the stress.

She disappeared and I was left all alone. It was what I wanted, but I felt a strange emptiness. I gently rocked back and forth and listened to the water and the birds. It was the kind of relaxation I needed after such a long, horrible year. I had to smile at the thought of my dear ex-wife calling and attempting to reach me. I hadn't mentioned I was going off the grid. She would call over and over. I could just imagine her anger. She'd been pulling my strings for fifteen years. It was about time I cut the ties.

"So over it," I muttered.

Her future husband could deal with her. He could have his life taken over and controlled by her. I almost felt sorry for the poor sap. Almost. Not entirely. He'd been fucking her while I was married to her. He got what he wanted. I still remembered the look on his face when he showed up at my headquarters with her. He acted like he'd won the gold medal. The man actually thought he had scored by landing Amanda. I just knew he was going to one day regret his decision. When that day came, I was going to be laughing my ass off. The only reason I didn't knock the guy out was because he saved me from an alimony payment. She couldn't make me pay alimony because she was already on her way down the aisle again before the ink even dried on our divorce papers.

I rose from the chair and made my way back to the dock. I thought about fishing, but what was the point? Oleg would show up at just the wrong time. I would save the fish and my bottle of scotch for when I could come back alone. I sat on the edge of the dock and watched the tiny little fish swimming in the shallow water. The sun beat down on my neck and shoulders. The idea to dive into the water was very tempting, but I didn't want to get my clothes wet before my departure. Going naked wasn't an option in case our grizzly captain came back.

Instead, I sat and waited. And waited some more. There was no sign of Oleg anywhere. No sign of anyone. No boats. No people. Nothing. My temporary roommate was probably on the other side of the island that boasted twenty acres of privacy. It felt a lot bigger with all the trees and foliage that created some pretty handy privacy screens. I waited around the dock for an hour before heading back up to the cottage. I knocked on the door to avoid having another encounter that would leave her pissed and questioning my presence.

"Hello? Gabby are you here?"

There was no answer. I dared to venture to check the bedroom. "Gabby are you in here?"

The place was empty. She was obviously still out on her walk. With nothing better to do, I grabbed one of the books from the shelf. It was some action story set in World War II. I wasn't much of a reader, but it seemed like a good way to pass the time. I read a few chapters before dropping the book on the couch. I couldn't get into the story. I kept wondering where she was. She'd been gone a while. Should I be worried about her? I didn't exactly consider the woman a friend, but she was a woman alone on an island.

She was likely watching and waiting for me to leave. That was pretty sad. She hated me enough to stay away from the cabin she was fighting so hard for. I stepped onto the porch and felt the change in weather. There was definitely a storm coming. I could see dark clouds on the horizon. That alone might be enough to keep Oleg away. Or maybe he'd come out to check on us. If I left, she would be out here by herself. What if it was a violent storm? What if something happened and she was out here by herself?

As much as I didn't want her to be alone, I had to think about what it would mean if I stayed. She'd keep me outside. I was all about roughing it, but I didn't really care to ride out a hurricane on an exposed beach either. Quite the conundrum.

I flopped back down on the couch and picked up the book again. I was just getting to the action when the door opened. I looked up just as she looked at me and screamed. "What the hell!"

"Good to see you as well," I said with a tight smile and closed the book.

"Why are you still here?" she asked in a way that made her sound like she was in actual pain.

I made a big show of sighing. "Because I don't want to drown. How many times do I need to say this?"

"You know what I mean," she snapped. She had her hands on her hips in that bossy manner once again. "You're still here. I stayed gone all day. I thought you would be gone."

"Did you see or hear a boat?" I asked pointedly.

"No, but I was on the other side of the island," she said. "I assumed you would be gone."

"Careful," I warned with a smile. "Assuming just makes an ass out of you."

"If I remember correctly, it makes an ass out of you as well," she shot back.

"Oleg isn't here," I said. "He didn't show up. I waited out there for a quite a while. I even got a little sunburned."

"Were you even out there very long?" she asked. "What if he showed up while you were sitting in here reading your book?"

"My ears work just fine," I said. "I didn't hear him. Besides, I'm sure he would have made his presence known. He would come to the door. He didn't. He never showed up. I guess he assumed we figured out a compromise."

"There's that assume thing again," she said with a sigh.

"Look, I think we need to figure something out here," I said. "Oleg isn't going to show up here at dusk. There's a storm coming in."

"I'm not figuring anything out," she said. "I'm going to *my* room. Please be gone when I come back out."

"It doesn't work like that," I called out even as she walked away. Her answer was the door slamming.

I could really use a drink right about now. The woman was insufferable. The more attitude she threw out, the more I wanted to get the hell off the island. That was likely her hope. She wanted to make me miserable enough to swim back to the mainland. She was close to succeeding. As much as I wanted to get off the island and away from the surly and simultaneously sexy doctor, I didn't think it was happening today. I sure as hell didn't think it was fair that I was the one being pushed into the cold. The cottage was big enough for the both of us. I just needed to find a way to get that through to her. I'd take the couch. She could have the bedroom.

I heard the crack of thunder in the distance. There was no way she didn't see the clouds. She knew there was a storm coming. If she didn't, she had no business being on the island at all. I'd give her a few minutes to accept the fact I was still on the island. Then we were going to talk about the accommodations for tonight.

I could attempt to bribe her with kindness. With the number of bottles of wine lined up on the counter, I gathered she was a wine drinker. I sure as hell didn't put those on my grocery order. I could open a bottle of wine, pour her a glass and kill her with kindness. In the old days, I'd been told more than once I was very charming. That charming side of me had been buried for a long time. It was time to pull it out and dust it off.

She couldn't be completely immune to my charms, could she?

Chapter Eleven

Gabby

I paced the room for several minutes. This was not good. Not good at all. I couldn't be trapped on this island with him for another night. The whole time I was out walking, I thought about him. Those damn eyes. I had a real weakness for blue eyes, but his eyes were so much more than the blue I was used to seeing. I wasn't exactly a sexually active person, but damn if I didn't have a few small fantasies about riding a man like him. I let myself have those fantasies because I had convinced myself he was already gone. A bottle of wine and one of my slightly smutty books were supposed to be my date for the night.

Now, I had to deal with him. I needed to get this settled. Before I could have what I expected was going to be another difficult conversation, I needed to clean up. The humidity had been brutal. I felt like a sweaty pig, though the walk around the island had been amazing. The place was beautiful and so raw. I loved that, for the most part, the island was untouched by humans. I had scanned the beach for seashells and while I found some, I couldn't bring myself to take them. They belonged to the island. I inspected wildflowers, and even found some cool little hermit crabs burrowing into the sand. All in all, it had been a very enjoyable experience until I got back and realized he was still here.

I grabbed a fresh set of clothes and rushed across the hall to the bathroom. I took a three-minute shower and piled my hair into a messy bun before exiting the bathroom. The whole time I'd been out walking and exploring, I was hoping he would be gone. I felt incredibly selfish. I wanted the whole place to myself. He obviously had some rights to the place, but for this one time, I wanted to be completely selfish. All day, every single day I gave of myself. I gave to my patients and my fellow doctors. When nurses were upset and stressed, I comforted them. I gave up on-call sleeping rooms for exhausted nurses that just needed a few minutes. I didn't think this was too much to ask for.

I would have preferred him to be gone when I exited the bathroom, but I knew he would still be there. I didn't really like confrontation, but I could sense him. It was like I could feel his presence. Like we had some strange connection. I walked into the living room and sure enough, he was sitting on the couch with one foot propped on his knee. He looked so casual, like he belonged in this place. In my life. He didn't belong. He was an intruder.

"Feel better?" he asked.

"Yes."

"I know you aren't anxious to talk to me, but we need to talk," he said.

"I'm not sure there's anything more to say." I sighed and sat down in the single chair in the living room. Being in the same room with him was disconcerting. I couldn't explain what it was that upset me so much about him. I just felt like I had to be completely on guard. He was dangerous. Not in a physical way, but there was a red alert sounding in the back of my mind that this man had the power to make me feel things I didn't want to feel.

"I'm sure you noticed the clouds," he said. "Maybe you heard the thunder?"

I shrugged and pretended it wasn't a big deal. "So? That happens all the time. Are you afraid of a little thunder?"

"So, it's going to rain," he said.

"Yep," I said with a smile. "It probably is."

"Oleg isn't coming today," he stated, and dropped his foot from his knee as he leaned forward. "He's obviously decided not to come back until the next grocery run. That means we're stuck here. Together. Just the two of us. We're on this island for a week. Do not ask me to swim back to the mainland. I won't ask you to do it. It's much better if we just accept the fact we're both here."

"Don't say that," I groaned.

"I can say something else, but the facts remain unchanged."

"I don't want you here," I pouted. "This is just not how this is supposed to be happening. I don't want a man around. I don't want anyone around."

"You're not exactly a barrel of rosy sunshine," he said. "But we all have our crosses to bear. I don't particularly want you here either. But again, here we are without a paddle. Or a boat for that matter."

"I'm not sure what you're expecting from me," I said and threw up my arms. "I can't change the weather. I can't conjure up a boat. Someone screwed up and now we're stuck paying the price."

He scoffed. "If you try hard enough you might be able to wave a hand or chant or cast a spell. I'm sure stranger things have happened in your life."

My mouth dropped open. "Are you calling me a witch?"

"I didn't say that," he said with his lips quirking at the corners.

"But you insinuated it," I said.

"No, you suggested you couldn't conjure up a boat," he shrugged. "What do you normally conjure?"

"Very funny," I muttered.

"I'll take the couch," he said as if it was so normal.

"No!" I gasped. "Hell no!"

I shook my head. I couldn't share a house with a stranger. That was too weird. Too intrusive. I didn't know him. He could seem decent and then turn into a violent, crazy man as soon as we were trapped in the house together. Then again, he could turn into a violent man while he was outside the house. That wasn't the point. I had never lived with a man and didn't intend to start now. I was supposed to be on vacation.

"I'll remind you, I've been very, very generous," he said slowly. His eyes narrowed and for the first time, I sensed genuine anger. "I've done my best to stay out of your way. I've apologized for something that isn't my fault. I've tolerated your bitchy attitude. I've done nothing to upset you."

"You're sitting on my couch!" I shrieked.

"I bet you didn't play well with others when you were a kid, did you?" he smirked. "You need a hard, fast lesson on sharing. This isn't even sharing, technically. I paid to sit on this couch. I paid to use the kitchen and as a matter of fact, I paid to sleep in that bed. I'm not asking for you to give up the bed. I'm not asking you to hang out and entertain me. I'm simply suggesting we come up with a compromise. That's what adults do."

"I'm not sharing a house with you," I said again and actually stomped my foot which I immediately regretted.

"Too bad, sweetheart," he shot back. "I'm here. You're here. It's time to pull on your big girl panties and figure out how to work through a problem. For being a doctor, you seem to lack some very basic problem-solving skills."

"I understand we both paid for this place, but—"

He held up his hand. "You were here first. If I would have known I was going to be stranded on an island with a three-year-old, I would have brought toys. Maybe that would keep you occupied. I'm sure I can find a stick you could pretend is a doll or something."

"Don't you dare insult me," I said.

"Quit acting like a child. You've got a huge chip on your shoulder. I'm simply trying to figure something out. That's what adults do. When there is a problem, they sit down and figure it out. Two adults generally toss around solutions and then the grownups each give a little. It's what we call compromise. It's part of life."

"Do not talk down to me," I said with irritation. "I don't have to compromise. Not when I paid to have a nice vacation away from everyone on the planet. It's rude to assume I have to give up what I paid for."

"You don't say?" he smirked. "Please tell me more about what that's like. I mean, didn't I pay to come out here away from everyone? Most especially women with big attitudes."

The man had seemed so nice yesterday. Today, he was downright rude and obnoxious. I refused to accept responsibility for this situation. "You came out here knowing full well I was already here," I said and pointed a finger at him. "You thought you were going to sweet talk me or bully me into giving up the island so you can have it."

"That's not true," he argued.

"Yes, it is!" I said with the anger building. "What did you think you were going to accomplish by coming out here even after Oleg told you I was here? Did you really think I was just going to bow out and leave the place to you?"

That seemed to give him pause. "I was hoping we could work something out," he said. "I did and do plan on staying on the beach the bulk of the time. I'm perfectly happy to sleep out there. Tonight is different. There's a storm. Would you really have me out on the beach in the middle of a storm?"

That was a loaded question. "I think I saw a tarp in the small shed," I said.

His brows popped up. "A tarp?"

"Yes, a tarp. You could set it up like a tent."

He shot me a dirty look. "I'm supposed to live like a survivalist while you sit up here in this house?"

I gave him a tight smile. "I'm offering a compromise. That's what adults do, right?"

"I'm the one compromising," he growled. "You're barking orders and acting like the damn queen of the island. I'm the one being told to sleep out with the bugs. I'm not sure where you're compromising."

"I can't have you in here," I said again.

"I don't give a shit what you can and can't have," he growled and got to his feet. "Am I supposed to just wash away? Am I supposed to magically hang the tarp? Honestly, did you think this little idea of yours through at all?"

He made a lot of good points, but I wasn't about to tell him that. "There's a hammock out back," I said.

"And?"

"You can sleep in it. Then you won't have to worry about being washed out to sea."

He rolled his eyes. "You're pretty fucking generous."

He stomped past me and out the door. I wasn't sure what he was doing. I heard him muttering and followed him outside. He opened the small shed and pulled out the tarp and some rope. Still bitching under his breath, he walked around the cottage to the side of the house where a hammock had been strung between two trees.

I watched from the porch until he whipped his head around. "What?" he snapped. "Is this a problem? Would you prefer I move the hammock away from your precious bedroom? Am I too close?"

"No, I was just wondering what you were doing."

He cursed and looked up at the sky. "Go away," he finally said so quietly I barely heard him.

"Excuse me?"

"You heard me," he sighed. "Just leave me alone, please. I am doing what you wanted. I'm sleeping out here. I need to put together a tent. I don't need you bitching at me and critiquing what I'm doing. If you can do it better, feel free to do it and I'll take the bed."

"I wasn't critiquing," I said. "I was just watching."

He spun around. "Look, lady, you can't have it both ways. You either leave me the hell alone for real or you drop the bullshit and quit being such a bitch."

I hated being called a bitch. It was one of those things I found beyond reprehensible. "Enjoy the rain," I snapped. "I hope it pours."

"Anything is better than being trapped in that house with you," he called out as I walked away.

My parents would be mortified by my behavior. Truth be told, I was a little embarrassed myself. I couldn't seem to stop. I was not this person. I was acting like a spoiled brat. I didn't know why. It just seemed to spill out of me every time I opened my mouth around him. He infuriated me for no real reason.

I closed the cottage door and went into the kitchen to find something to eat and break into one of the bottles of wine. It wasn't like there was a large selection of food to choose from. The stuff I didn't recognized from my shopping list, I ignored. I didn't want to eat his food. Not even I was that rude. I sat down with the bowl of noodles and my glass of wine and heard the first sounds of rain starting to fall.

I was tempted to look outside but was afraid that would be the exact moment he caught me checking on him. Was he okay? Was he cold? How wet was it? What if it turned into a full-blown storm? I couldn't leave him out there in good conscience. I was already feeling bad enough as it was. If I was a big enough person, I could go out there and apologize for being so hasty and rude. I would invite him inside to sleep.

But I wasn't that big. If he was inside, we'd be forced to talk. If we talked, I would get to know him. What if I actually liked the guy? That was not what I needed right now. I needed this time alone to get my head straight. Getting mixed up with a man, even if it was just as an acquaintance, would be more than I could emotionally handle right now.

I chose to ignore him. I finished my noodles and washed the dishes I had used. I didn't miss the fact he'd washed our coffee cups. He was neat. I liked that. If he wanted to be a jerk, he could have left the dishes in the sink for me to take care of. He had even cleaned the coffee pot. I found myself smiling as I added a clean liner and coffee grounds to make it easy in the morning. It wasn't quite the Keurig I was used to, but it worked.

The rain outside hit the roof in a soothing ratatat sound. It was comfortable inside the cottage but just a little chilly. I went into the room and pulled on one of my hoodies. If I was chilly inside, what was he dealing with outside? Once again, guilt had me rethinking my hasty decision to kick him out. I casually looked out the window but saw nothing but blue tarp. He'd hung it from the trees to create a lean-to over the hammock. If the wind picked up, the rain would simply blow in at him.

"If it gets bad, I'll let him in," I told myself before settling in on the couch where he'd been.

I swore I could smell his manly scent on the fabric. That couldn't be right. I was imagining things. This was what happened when a healthy, somewhat young woman denied herself the pleasure of a man for too long. Add in the romance novel I'd been reading last night, and I was primed for longing.

The rain started to fall harder. He had to be cold. Should I offer him a blanket? That wouldn't do much good if it was wet. Despite what the man probably thought about me, I wasn't a total unfeeling bitch. I was concerned, which was why I got off the couch and stepped outside. The rain pelted against the porch cover. I walked to the edge and tried to peer into the man's tent. The tent I had relegated him to in a temper tantrum I was quickly coming to regret.

"Hello?" I called out. "Jake?"

There was no answer. I wondered if he was even in the damn tent. I didn't have my shoes on. I walked to the edge and tried to peer around the side. "Jake?"

"What?" his muffled growl came out.

"Uh, are you okay?" I asked what was probably one of the dumbest question ever.

"Leave me alone," he barked.

I was going to take that sound advice and went back inside the cottage. He was pissed. I couldn't really blame him. Feeling bad, I didn't lock the door in case the weather did turn nasty and he needed to come inside. I was going to call it an early night so I grabbed the book and headed for bed. Just in case the storm did turn wild, I slept in the shorts and tank. I wasn't planning on giving Jake another free peep show. As I laid in bed and listened to the rain dance on the roof, I hoped he was really okay out there. Fortunately, it didn't feel too cold.

"Sorry," I whispered into the dark.

I felt bad, but not bad enough to invite him in. I would just have to live with the guilt.

Chapter Twelve

Jake

I stared up and into darkness. It was very dark. This was where the term pitch black applied. I could barely see my hand in front of my face. She'd shut off the lights in the cottage a bit ago. I had a flashlight, but turning it on was pointless. What was I going to look at, the dark sky? It was strange, but the rain beating on the tarp was very soothing. It took me back to better days. Days before life got complicated. The hammock was actually very comfortable as well. I had one in my backyard at home, but I realized I didn't spend nearly enough time in the thing. I was going to remedy that.

The sleeping bag kept me plenty warm, and the tarp kept me dry. With the way I had the lean-to set up, I had an amazing view of the water and the sky. Not that I could see the water, but every time there was a flash of lightning, I got a great view. Mother Nature was terrifying and beautiful at the same time. I was always in awe of the power nature wielded. Humans thought they ran the earth, but we were nothing compared to Mother Nature. She was the true power. She ruled.

The storm wasn't as bad as I thought it would be, which was good for me. Initially, I'd been pissed that she forced me to sleep outside. It wasn't that I was afraid of sleeping outside in the middle of a storm, been there, done that. It was the fact she'd been so damn selfish. This could have easily been a very dangerous situation. It could have been bad, and I didn't think she'd give a shit. Her selfishness infuriated me. But that wasn't my problem. She could do whatever the hell she wanted. I was going to make the most of the time I had here. In fact, sleeping outside like this was exactly what I'd had in mind. It just sucked her negative energy was bringing down my mood. Unfortunately for her, I had a lot of experience dealing with soul-sucking women that wanted to make my life miserable. I was an expert at ignoring the negative energy. I drifted off to sleep to the soothing sound of the rain and the waves without a care in the world. The hammock was like floating on a cloud. Despite the circumstances, I was actually very happy.

When I woke the next morning, the sun had just broken free of the horizon. It was going to be a good day. I climbed out of the hammock and grabbed one of the bottles of water. I didn't need coffee to get my day started. I had fresh air and fishing. Loaded with bait and a fishing pole, I headed down to the dock. Fishing from the shore was difficult. The dock was the perfect spot. I set up my pole and cast out the line. The peacefulness after a storm was incredible.

It wasn't long before I caught the first fish. I stayed out several hours enjoying the peacefulness. Fishing was about so much more than just catching fish. It was the time for a man to contemplate and all the decisions he had made and needed to make in the future. The whole point of this vacation was for me to do exactly this. I wasn't supposed to have to worry about anything or anyone. I definitely didn't want to have to worry about the surly woman back at the cottage.

It was pretty clear we were going to be stuck together for the next several days. I figured it would be better to make it as peaceful as possible. I would avoid her as much as I could. If I stayed out of her way and vice versa, maybe we could make this thing work.

My stomach growled and I decided to call it good. I had four good size fish and I could practically taste the meat in my mouth. I collected my things and picked up the basket with the fish fillets I had already cut up. I carried my bounty back to the fire ring I had made on the beach the first night. After collecting some firewood, I attempted to get a fire going. I tried like hell to get the wood to ignite, but it was pointless. The wood was soaked.

I wasn't about to let the fish go to waste. Once again, I collected my things and headed up to the cottage. I knocked on the front door, which still pissed me off. Technically, I had rented the place. For me to have to knock to go in was frustrating. When she didn't answer, I pushed the door open and looked around. It was empty. Hopefully, that meant she was out exploring again. Maybe she was laying nude on the beach somewhere. I quickly dismissed the thought. I didn't need to be thinking about her naked. That would only make this situation so much worse than it already was. Certain she wasn't home, I headed for the kitchen and started cooking the fish. Since I had an actual kitchen and the groceries I had ordered, I decided to make it a real meal.

I was stirring the rice I was making to go with the fish when I heard the door open. "Seriously?" she snapped.

I rolled my eyes before turning around. "What now?"

"When are you going to stop walking in like you own the place?" she snapped.

"I suppose the same time you do," I shot back.

"What are you talking about? What are you doing? Why are you in the kitchen? I thought we agreed I was keeping the cottage and you were going to roam about the island until Oleg came back."

"You mean until Oleg comes to my rescue?" I said before turning back to the rice.

"You can't—"

"Stop," I said and cut her off before she could lay into yet another lecture. I was about sick of her lectures saying the same thing over and over. "Just stop. I'm making lunch. I'm more than happy to share my catch with you."

"Why here?" she asked with a sigh.

"Because you might not be aware of this, but it rained last night. A lot. I tried to stay out of your precious bubble, but I'm fucking hungry. I want to eat my lunch in peace. If I give you a plate, will you please just give me thirty minutes of peace and quiet?"

She didn't respond. I turned around to see if she was still in the room. The expression on her face told me I might have gone a step too far. I immediately felt like a dick. I was usually much calmer. I rarely let anyone get under my skin. I blamed it on the hunger. I was famished. The last couple of days had been stressful and I wasn't eating much. I just needed to sit down and eat a real meal without being nagged to death. A man could only take so much.

"I'm sorry," I said with a sigh. "Can we please just start over?" I asked.

"Again?" she asked with a raised brow.

"Yes, please."

"What are you making?" she asked and for the first time since I'd met her on the beach, I didn't hear derision.

"Fresh caught fish and wild rice," I said.

"Really?" she asked with genuine surprise. "Like, you actually caught the fish?"

"They sure as hell didn't swim into the pan," I teased.

She moved to stand next to me in front of the stove. "It smells good."

"It's going to taste just as good," I promised.

"Can I do anything?"

"There's a lemon in the fridge, can you slice it into wedges, please?" I asked her.

It was a little like walking into the twilight zone. She was being nice. I didn't dare do anything to make her pissed at me again. I was going to be nice as well.

"Here you go," she said and held out a small plate with the wedges on it.

"Thank you."

I squeezed some of the lemon juice over the fish and listened to the sizzle. There was an awkward silence between us. If we were going to live together for the next five days, we needed to clear the air. I didn't want the tension. It was bad energy.

"I don't think Oleg is coming back," I said.

"Me either," she said and sounded none too happy about it.

"I know we've been at odds, but I think we can agree there isn't anything we can do about the situation," I said calmly. With her, I wasn't sure when she would change her mind and decide to hate me again.

"I know."

"I don't want to ruin your vacation," I told her. "I think we've both got our own shit to work through. We came here with a purpose to be alone and get our heads straight. I don't want to deny you your peace. I'd like you to do the same for me."

"Okay, and how do we do that?" she asked.

"We stay out of one another's way," I said. "I don't mind sleeping outside."

"What about last night?" she asked. "Was it terrible?"

"No," I answered immediately. "It wasn't bad."

"Did you get wet?" she asked hesitantly.

"Nope. A little, but not enough to make it miserable. I stayed warm enough in my bag."

"Good."

"The wood is wet after the rain last night," I told her. "It's why I had to use the stove. If you want to work out some kind of schedule, I'd be cool with that. The shower as well."

"Jake, I want to apologize for being so difficult earlier," she said. "I just, well, you're a surprise. I had this idea of how this vacation was going to go. Then it kind of imploded."

"Trust me, I get it," I said. "I wasn't expecting company either. There's no reason to let this ruin both our vacations. We'll make the most of this week. Once Oleg comes back, I'll go back with him. You'll have the whole place to yourself again."

"I am sorry this got so messed up," she said. "It's pretty unbelievable this happened."

"You're okay with me using the kitchen?" I asked. "When I can, I'll use an open fire."

"I guess I kind of have to be okay with it," she said with a shrug.

That wasn't exactly an enthusiastic agreement, but it was better than the usual bullshit. "I'll stay out of your way."

"Thanks," she said. "If you happen to make extra, I wouldn't mind eating the leftovers."

I grinned and looked over at her. "You mean you want me to make you dinner? Lunch?"

"I'm saying there's no reason for food to go to waste."

I looked at her and did a mental catalog of the groceries I had seen in the cupboard. There were plenty of ready-to-eat things. "Do you know how to cook?" I asked her.

"Of course, I do," she snapped.

I raised an eyebrow. "Is that why you're stocked up on cup-of-soup and instant rice packets?"

"I—"

I wanted to laugh but I didn't dare ruin the newfound peace we'd found. "It's cool," I said.

"Do you cook a lot?" she asked.

"I cook enough," I answered.

"Has it always been that way?" she questioned.

"What? Me cooking?"

"Yes," she nodded.

"I think it's something I taught myself," I told her. "If I was hungry, I had to cook something."

She nodded but didn't say anything. I didn't want to spill my guts just yet. We weren't exactly friends. "Can you grab a couple of plates?" I asked her.

She moved to the cupboard and placed them on the counter. "Anything else?"

"Nah, have a seat," I told her. "This will be done in a few minutes."

"Thanks."

She sat down at the table while I finished the meal. It had been a long time since I cooked for anyone. Amanda didn't care for my cooking. I was convinced it had nothing to do with my cooking and more about the fact she couldn't cook. I never tried to insult her or make her feel inadequate because she couldn't cook. I thought it was me being nice. She thought it was me being an asshole. I should have known the relationship was doomed. But, stupid me, I kept trying. I wanted to make her happy. I thought learning how to cook some of her favorite meals was the way to do that. She preferred to order in or go out to expensive restaurants. She wanted to be seen. I just wanted to eat.

Chapter Thirteen

Gabby

I watched him move around the kitchen. He was comfortable in the kitchen and from the way that fish looked and smelled, he was a talented cook as well. Jake was the total package. He was hot as hell. Apparently, he was very capable. And now he cooked. There had to be something about him that was terrible. This was not okay. I couldn't be trapped on an island with the hottest guy on the planet. I was only human.

For one brief second, I let myself think about a week with him. Like really with him. It was the perfect scenario. Didn't every woman want to be stranded with the sexiest man alive? Granted, I wasn't sure what his relationship situation was like back home, but he didn't seem to be attached to anyone. If he was, he didn't act like it. Did I really want a man who would cheat on his girlfriend?

I took a giant mental step back. I had veered off the path somewhere and gone down a road that didn't exist. There was nothing to say this man was even remotely attracted to me. We'd been at each other's throats since he arrived. But then, here he was, making me lunch. The guy wasn't so bad. This whole vacation could have been very different so far, had I just given him a chance. I had him within my reach, and I kept pushing him away. Hell, I was doing a lot more than that. I had turned into a she-devil. Now I really felt bad watching him cook me a meal.

He brought me a plate at the table with a fork and everything. "There you go," he said and walked back to the stove.

I inhaled the scent and found myself absolutely starving. I noticed him collecting some napkins and a fork instead of putting them on the table. "Are you eating?" I asked.

"I'll eat outside," he said and grabbed his own plate.

"You don't have to do that," I said. "I mean, if you want to, I won't stop you, but don't feel like you have to. I wouldn't mind you having a seat here."

He smirked and stood next to the table. "You're sure?" he asked. "I don't want to overstay my welcome. This is good. I don't want to disrupt a good thing."

"Please, have a seat," I said.

He sat down and only then I felt like I could take my first bite. I was dying to dig in. It smelled amazing and looked just as good. He watched as I took my first bite. He cut off his own piece. "Well?" he asked.

"It's delicious," I said. The fish was moist and flaky, and the flavor was amazing. He was a talented cook.

"You're just saying that," he laughed.

"No, I'm not. This is really good." I took another bite. "This is restaurant quality good."

"Thank you," he said, and took his own bite.

"Do you do a lot of fishing?" I asked conversationally.

"Not as much as I'd like to," he answered. "If I could, I think I would fish for all my meals. Maybe not the same kind of fish, but I enjoy catching my food and then eating it fresh. Nothing beats that feeling of satisfaction."

"Is that why you came out here?" I asked. "You wanted to live off the land and test your survivor skills?" The last was supposed to be a jest. I wanted him to see I didn't always have to act like a total jerk.

He slowly nodded. "Basically. I'm not great at hunting. I can do it, but I think I prefer a little less blood."

"Where did you say you lived?" I asked the question I was sure we had covered once. Unfortunately, our first few interactions weren't great, and my adrenaline had been pumping. It was hard to really hear anyone when you were trying to figure out how to throw them off an island.

"Maine," he answered. "Just outside of Bangor."

"That's right," I nodded. "Do you like it there?"

"I do," he said.

I liked the conversation. It was all very basic, but we were communicating instead of screaming at one another. This was a good thing. I hoped we could keep it up. "I flew into Bangor and then caught a ride out here. It seemed like a nice place, very quaint and old-fashioned."

He smiled and nodded. "That's what brought me to the place."

"From where?" I asked with curiosity.

"New York," he answered and the look on his face said it all.

"The city?"

"Manhattan," he nodded.

"You didn't like it?" I pushed.

"It was okay for a while," he said. "I loved living there in the beginning, but as I got older, I wanted to get back to a slower way of life. I wanted to slow down and breathe clean air. I wanted to be able to jump in my car and drive somewhere without hearing blaring horns and sirens."

"Did you grow up in the city?" I continued my line of questioning.

He slowly shook his head. "No. Upstate in an average town with average people. I grew up hunting and fishing with my dad. We went camping a lot. It was all very normal."

"Sounds like a nice childhood," I said with a smile.

"What about you? You said you were from LA. Always been?"

I slowly nodded. "Always. My parents were Beverly Hills doctors. I went to medical school in California. I've always been there."

"Do you like it there?" he asked me.

"I do," I said with a finality I hadn't expected. "I love the weather and the ocean. I like the different people and there is always something going on. Not that I have time to do anything, but I know there will always be a concert or show I could go to if I wanted to. I love the palm trees and the sun."

He laughed with those gorgeous blue eyes twinkling. "You sound like you work for the tourism department."

"I could," I replied. "I know just about every inch of southern California. Not a lot about the northern half of the state though."

"What brought you all the way out here?" he asked. "How did you find this place?"

I had to laugh. "Google. Lots of Googling."

"You didn't want to stay in the state you love?" he teased.

"Nope. I wanted to get as far away as I could. I thought about Hawaii, but too many tourists. I just wanted to see something new and experience something different. I guess there is such a thing as too much of a good thing."

"Did you search for an island retreat?" he asked. "How did you find this one particular island on the other side of the country? I know they don't do a lot of advertising for this place and on the vacation rental searches, it barely makes the cut."

"Honestly, it kind of just happened," I told him. "I didn't know where I wanted to go. I just started looking for cabins in the woods and stuff like that. The cottage appeared in one of my searches. At first, I laughed at the idea. I was like, no way. I wanted to be alone, but a deserted island seemed extreme."

"And yet, here you are."

"Yeah, things changed, and I realized this was exactly what I needed," I said. "I did more research and felt confident I would be okay on my own. I researched the weather patterns and even wildlife. Nothing seemed too scary. What about you? How did you end up here?"

"Same story, basically," he said. "I was at a point in my life where I knew I had to reset. I needed to start fresh. I actually knew about this place from some locals. I looked it up and decided it was where I needed to be."

"A reset," I nodded. "That's a good way to put it. I think that's what I'm doing. I'm trying to reset my life. Not a total reset of my life, but of me. Who I am and what I'm doing with my life."

"Why?" he asked casually. "That sounds like the kind of thing you realize after a life-changing event."

I figured I could tell him without really telling him anything too personal. "I was working too hard."

"You said you were a doctor?"

"Yes," I nodded. "I did dual credit when I was in high school. I graduated with my high school degree and my associate's degree at the same time. I was on a fast track through medical school. Got into my residency and just kept going. I never took a minute to just breathe. I did summer classes and volunteered at the free clinic. It has been nonstop from the moment I hit seventh grade. My parents were overachievers. I was lucky enough to inherit that gene."

"You're pretty young to be a doctor," he said.

"Like I said, I've been busting my ass forever," I said. "You?"

"Me?"

"Are you out here because you were overworked?" I asked.

He wrinkled his nose. "Yes and no. I was overworked but I have since stepped away from the day to day that kept me at the office twelve hours a day. I stepped away and gave up the bulk of the control to my COO. I still keep an eye on things and I'm handling expansion and stuff like that."

"What is your business?" I asked him.

"I own a chain of sporting goods stores," he said.

"Oh," I said with surprise. "Successful?"

He grinned with a twinkle in his eyes. "You could say that. I'm not one of the biggest chains in the country, but I do all right. I like that we're a small business. We have a handful of stores in the northeast but that might change soon."

"You're taking a vacation to figure out how you can work harder?" I joked.

He chuckled. "Yes and no. I needed to get away to clear my head. Reset and reexamine my priorities."

I nodded as he talked. "Reset. I like that."

"What about your personal life?" he asked.

"What about it?"

"I guess the first question would be, do you have one?"

I threw my head back and laughed. "Honestly, no."

"No boyfriend?" he questioned.

"No boyfriend," I said. "I guess you could say that's a symptom of my work ethic. I've worked too much. I've isolated myself. I need to start living in the real world."

He laughed and took a drink from the bottle of water. "So, you chose a deserted island for a vacation."

I pulled a face. "You make a good point, but I wasn't taking a vacation to find a boyfriend. I was taking a vacation to give myself a break from myself. I had to step back and give myself a minute to think. To figure out what my priorities are."

"Are you questioning your decision to become a doctor?" he asked.

"No!" I gasped. "Definitely not. I like my life and all that, but I've recently been questioning my choices I guess you could say. I need a minute to reassess."

"Me too," he agreed. "I guess we're two people reassessing."

"I guess so."

We finished our lunch and when he started to clean up, I stopped him. "I'll do it," I told him. "You literally caught our meal and cooked it. I can clean up."

He nodded. "I get it. I'll go."

"What are you going to do?" I asked. "I mean, with your day."

"I think I'm going to go for a swim and then try and collect some dry firewood," he said.

"And you're just going to hang out on the beach?" I questioned.

"Yes," he said with a laugh. "It's all I want to do. I didn't come out here for a touristy vacation. I'm here to be with my own company. I have a couple of books and I was thinking about picking up an old habit again."

"What old habit?" I asked.

He actually looked a little embarrassed. "Whittling."

"What?"

"Whittling," he said again. "Wood carving."

"You whittle?"

"You seem surprised," he laughed.

"I just, well, I guess it's not a hobby I imagine a guy like you participating in," I said.

"What kind of hobby do you think I should be involved in?"

I shrugged. "Working out? Running? Golfing?"

He laughed again. "While I do enjoy all those things, I'm not a one trick pony. I like to do other things. Thanks for letting me use the kitchen. I'll see you around—maybe. Hopefully not."

"Hopefully not?"

"Because we're keeping our distance," he said.

"Oh, yeah, right," I nodded. "Okay, well, if you need anything, just knock. Please knock."

"Got it," he said and walked out of the cottage.

I walked to the window and watched him head through the trees. I cursed the view. It wasn't totally clear. He was somewhat visible as he headed towards the same spot he'd been the first night. I drifted away from the window and cleaned up the kitchen. Even though I told myself not to do it, I went back to the window to take a little peek. There was a small fire burning and I could make out his sleeping bag and a beach chair beside the fire.

He came into view carrying a stack of wood. I watched him drop it and then to my surprise and pleasure, he pulled off his shirt and tossed it on the sand. Then he lost the cargo shorts he'd been wearing. "Don't do it," I whispered.

Do it.

He turned and looked over his shoulder almost directly at me. He was staring in my direction, but I knew he couldn't actually see me. Could he? He took a few steps towards the water and then dropped the boxers.

"No way!" I shrieked.

He dove under the water and disappeared. I couldn't look away. I was glued to the window. He popped up and then dove under once again. I watched him swim before he turned and started walking out of the water.

"Look away, Gabby," I murmured. "Look away. This is a total violation of his privacy."

Despite knowing what was right, I couldn't look away. I was glued to the scene unfolding in front of me. His gaze looked towards me once again. I knew he saw me watching him. I quickly turned around and flopped on the couch. That was just a little embarrassing.

Chapter Fourteen

Jake

I laid in my bag and couldn't stop smiling. She'd been watching. I had caught her looking. At least, I thought I had. I was pretty certain there was a figure in the window when I came out of the water. She could pretend to hate me all she wanted, but there was a spark. I wasn't going to try and fool myself into thinking there was anything between us or ever would be, but there was the spark of a human inside that woman's beautiful body.

She could be cold and ruthless, but for the first time this afternoon, I saw a side of her that proved she was human. She was a woman with walls. I could totally get that. It was an effective way to protect oneself. I wish I would have been better with walls. Unfortunately, I was not a man who did walls. I was just out there to be stomped all over.

It was a nice, calm night. The sky above me was littered with stars. It was stunning. I wished I was talented enough to take a picture of it, but a picture wouldn't do this view justice. This was the kind of view that you had to carry with you in the back of your mind. When I was having a bad day or Amanda was giving me hell, I was going to close my eyes and remember this picture.

I wondered what Gabby was doing. Reading a book? Taking a bath? It didn't matter. I was here for me. I had to stop thinking about her and what she was or wasn't doing. The gentle sound of the waves sent me back in time. Back to a time I didn't mind remembering. It wasn't necessarily a good memory, but one that I wanted to keep at the forefront because it was a life lesson. I let myself drift into the memory.

"Damn, I hate that smell," Amanda complained as I carried our bags into the small house on the beach we had rented for our honeymoon.

"It's the ocean, baby," I said with a laugh.

"It smells like nasty fish," she retorted. "I'm closing the windows. I hope this place has some air fresheners. I cannot spend an entire week here. It's musty. Do you smell that? Like dirty socks and dead fish."

I dropped our suitcases and pulled her into my arms. "It smells like the ocean," I said. "You're just used to the smell of exhaust and trash. This is what fresh air smells like."

She pouted in the prettiest way. I gave her a quick kiss. "You're so good to me," she said with a little smile. "I'm freaking out and you're trying to calm me down."

"I want us to enjoy this week," I told her. "One whole week with just the two of us. No one is going to bother us. It's just me and you. It's been too long since we got to just be us. We don't have to go out with friends and be the perfect couple. We don't have to schmooze business investors. It's just Jake and Amanda, those two crazy kids who fell in love a couple of years ago."

"I know," she said with not as much enthusiasm as I hoped. "I'm just tired. It was a long drive. I want to be here with you. We need this. I just wish we could have flown to shorten the travel time. I hate traveling in the car."

The drive had been three hours. I understood this wasn't her dream honeymoon, but it was what we could afford, and I was so happy to have my bride away from the city. Away from her job and all the damn clients that constantly called her. She was my financial advisor and I had never called her that many times. We always said we were going to take a week off, but it never happened. I wanted to show her the other side of me. The man beyond the athlete and now business owner. She just didn't seem to care for that part of me.

"Why don't you go change?" I said. "I'll pour us some of that fancy champagne we got from the Michaelsons. We'll sit down and just relax."

"Fine," she said.

I followed her into the bedroom with our suitcases. She spun around to look at me with disgust on her face. "I thought this was a suite?"

"It's a cabin," I said. "It's a master suite because the bathroom is attached."

She forced a smile, but I saw the look of disappointment in her eyes. "You're right. I'm being too critical. I cannot wait until we get to buy our first apartment. As soon as this year is behind us, I know the profits are going to start rolling in. I'm thinking something overlooking the park. At least three bedrooms. We have to have a doorman."

"Babe, no shop talk," I said. "We agreed we weren't going to talk shop."

Amanda was spending the money we had yet to make.

"Okay, okay," she held up her hands. She gave me another kiss before pushing me out of the room.

I opened the bottle of champagne and poured us each a glass. While she changed, I stepped out onto the front porch of the cabin. There was an odor. I would give her that, but I could still smell the freshness of the air. I had been craving the ocean for two years. For two long years, Amanda and I had been building my company. She insisted on working all the time. We managed to plan a wedding, a very small affair, but that was it. Amanda was the motivation in this adventure. She had pulled strings and reached out to connections to get the capital we needed to start the business.

Technically, I had the capital, but she said I needed more. I was leaving it to the expert. She knew what she was talking about. I was just the guy with the startup money and the name. My Olympic bronze gave me some credibility. At least that's what she said. That's why she insisted we bust ass and move fast before my name faded from people's memories.

I wasn't as excited to start a business, but she was very convincing. And I loved the woman. I checked the time and realized she'd been in the bedroom for quite a while. I left the porch and walked to the bedroom. I listened at the door and thought I heard her talking. I pushed open the door and found her on the phone with her back to me.

"I know," she whispered. "It's okay. I'll be back in a few days. I'll call you as soon as I'm home."

"Amanda?" I said her name.

She jumped and spun around and actually attempted to hide the phone.

"Jake!"

"Who was that?" I asked.

"What? Who?"

"On the phone," I said.

"Oh, it was Geri," she said nonchalantly. "She had a question about a client."

"Doesn't she know we're on our honeymoon?" I asked. Somewhere in the back of my mind, there was an uneasy feeling. I pushed it away.

"I'm sorry," she said and kissed me. She kissed me until I forgot all about the phone call. All I could think about was my lovely bride. She kept me in bed and thoroughly satisfied for the rest of the day. I was a man in love. I didn't care about anything except being with my beautiful lady. We were bound to have some misunderstandings and rough times. I didn't care. I loved her and I was in it for the long run. I was determined to make the marriage work.

"Damn fool," I muttered as I landed firmly back in reality.

The day I found her in bed with her now boyfriend, every little moment and incident came flooding back. The honeymoon had been a red flag and I was such a complete, lovesick fool, I ignored the signs. Those little moments had plagued our entire marriage. She always had an explanation and a reason. I never questioned her. I should have, but I just wanted to keep the peace and chose to play dumb. It was why I made myself relive those moments. I needed to get better at reading people. I had to start listening to my instincts.

The first day of our honeymoon was a preview of the last thirteen years of my life. All the sneaky phone calls and the late nights at work. She often had overnight business trips. I never questioned her. She acted like she loved me. I knew I loved her. We got along for the most part. Our marriage was uneventful, to say the least. We both worked a lot but when we did see each other, it was good. Maybe good was an exaggeration. It was decent. We had enough in common to have something to talk about when we were together. It was easier to talk about the business or her many social events than to talk about us.

Looking back, I realized I was going through the motions. I loved her, but I hadn't been in love with Amanda for a long, long time. I was in love with the idea of being married to someone who could be my partner in life. Unfortunately, she saw me as her personal bank account. Every time she wanted something, I bought it. I spoiled her. It was me trying to buy her love. Boy, did that backfire.

The sex had fizzled a few years into the marriage. I couldn't even remember what sex was like with her. We started out hot and heavy. I remembered the days I thought I would die if I didn't get to take her to bed. I had been a horny nineteen-year-old kid in love. Sex pretty much dominated my thoughts. She used that to her advantage. I was malleable and would have done anything for her to get the chance to be with her. The sex got lame and I didn't care enough to try. That was another red flag. I should have known she was getting it somewhere else. It was the last thought I had before sleep claimed me.

When I woke the next morning, I was resigned to the fact Oleg wasn't coming until Monday. I accepted it and made the best of things. We spent the next few days seeing each other in passing and exchanging pleasantries, but nothing more. I occasionally used the kitchen and showered when she was out taking a walk. She made sure to avoid me. I didn't mind. It was better we didn't talk to one another. I didn't want to risk pissing her off in some way and inciting her wrath once again. What we had going on was so much better. The stay on the island was actually enjoyable. I didn't even care that I didn't get to sleep in a bed. Last night, I slept in the hammock, and it had been pure heaven.

Tonight, was my last night on the island. Tomorrow, Oleg would show up and I would have to say goodbye and keep to our agreement. The bottle of scotch was still in my bag. I told myself I was going to save it until I could come back. But I wasn't sure I was going to come back.

The novelty had worn off. The bloom had been plucked. I was going to find another place to take my long vacation. This wasn't going to work for me anymore. As soon as I got home, I would start my search for another island retreat.

I went about settling in for my last night. I planned on being good and hungover when Oleg showed up tomorrow. Then it would be my own bed tomorrow night. My week of island living would be over. I pulled the bottle from my bag and stared at it for several seconds. She was up there by herself. She would have the next three weeks to be alone. Tonight, we could celebrate my departure.

I carried the bottle up to the cottage and knocked on the door. She opened it wearing the usual tank top and shorts she always wore. I could see the hint of her bikini string poking out from under the strap.

"Hey," she greeted.

"This is it," I said.

"What's it?"

"This is the last night on the island for me," I told her. "I was thinking I'd go out in style. I've been saving this bottle of scotch for a while. I had planned on busting into it the first night, but it just didn't feel right."

"And tonight does?" she asked. "Do you want a glass?"

I smirked. "I don't want a glass. Do you want to drink with me?"

"Um—"

"You get to celebrate the fact I'm leaving," I said. "I get to drown my sorrows because I'm leaving. It's a two for one kind of thing."

If she said no, I was going to break into the bottle anyway. If she said yes, then my night would be just a little better. Either way, I was drinking the damn scotch. I was tired of carrying it around.

Chapter Fifteen

Gabby

There were times when you knew an idea was just plain bad. Busting into a bottle of what appeared to be very old, expensive scotch was a bad idea. We both knew it, yet here we were contemplating doing it anyway. In the pro column, he was leaving tomorrow. That was about it.

"Okay," I heard myself say. The against column had been completely ignored on purpose. I didn't want to talk myself out of this bad decision. "But can I use a glass?"

He grinned. "If you insist."

I gestured for him to come inside and grabbed two glasses. He poured us each half a glass before lifting his. "To my last night on the island," he said.

I smiled and lifted mine. "To my first night being alone on the island."

He laughed and took a drink. I took my first drink and had to close my eyes. It burned all the way down, but it wasn't terrible. "Well?" he asked.

"It's good," I lied.

"Are you a drinker?" he asked. "Beyond the wine."

"Not really."

"Then you better not try to keep up with me," he teased. "I'd hate for you to get wasted."

"It's not like either of us has to drive home," I laughed.

"True, but drunk girls tend to get a little frisky around me," he said and flashed that panty-dropping grin.

I rolled my eyes. "I think it might take a little more than that to get me to fall for your charms."

"I'll keep that in mind."

We moved to sit out on the porch. "Seriously, have you ever seen anything so beautiful?" he asked as the sky faded to bright oranges and pinks.

"No," I answered. "Obviously, being on the west coast, we have some pretty spectacular sunsets, but this is different. I am in love with the rawness of this place."

"Me too," he said.

"Are you going to come back next month?" I asked him.

He took a drink and appeared thoughtful. "I don't think so."

"What? Why not?"

"I think the novelty has worn off," he answered.

"Because of me?" I questioned.

"Nah, not really," he said without really convincing me. "I just think the bloom has faded."

"Are you going to take the rest of the vacation you said you needed?"

"I think so," he nodded.

"But you're not sure."

"I'm not sure if I truly need it," he said. "I thought I did, but running from my life isn't going to resolve anything."

"And you were running?"

"No," he said. "I don't know. I needed to get my head together and the last week has helped me do that. I think I might stick with what I know and love and rent a cabin in the woods."

I felt a little guilty for ruining his vacation. "Do you feel like you've resolved the issues that were bothering you?"

He smirked. "We're adults. Are any of our issues every fully resolved?"

"Good point," I laughed. "You mentioned you spent time with your father, does that mean you had a decent childhood?"

"I had a great childhood," he said. "My baggage has nothing to do with my folks. They are good, hard-working people."

"They're still around?"

"Yes," he nodded again. "My dad is a carpenter and still takes orders for custom pieces. My mom was a stay-at-home mom aka, my chauffer. She drove me all over the place."

"Ah, you were one of those kids that played sports," I said. "That makes sense."

"I was."

He was holding something back. I turned my head and looked at him. "Football?"

"I played a little football in junior high, but I couldn't keep up with football practice in high school and my track practice."

I couldn't help it. My lip curled. "Track? You ran track?"

His deep laughter made the hairs on the back of my neck stand up. It was rich and powerful and felt like I was being caressed. "Yes and no. I did the javelin throw."

"Isn't that the really big stick?" I asked.

He laughed again. "Something like that."

"I just don't see it," I said. "I pegged you for football or maybe baseball."

"I did like those sports, but I excelled at the javelin," he said. "I liked it being a solo activity. I had no one to blame for myself if I failed. When I succeeded, I knew that was all me as well."

"You sound like you've been a loner for a while," I said.

"I guess I have." He shrugged. "I like personal responsibility."

"So, were you any good at the javelin?"

He offered a cocky smirk. "You could say that."

"Is there like a Superbowl or something to decide who's the best?"

He laughed again. "Yeah, there's a little something we like to call the Olympic games."

I rolled my eyes. "Well, all sports have the Olympics. Once you're out of high school, it's over, right?"

He cleared his throat. "For some, sure. Some go on to college on track scholarships and compete at that level."

"Did you do that?"

He slowly shook his head. "No. I did go but I didn't run track at school. I was on a team."

"A team?"

"The US team," he said.

I didn't get it. "Oh. That's cool. Did you guys compete against other countries? I'm sorry, I know so little about this stuff. I know football and basketball."

"We did compete against other countries," he said with that cocky grin again. "At the Olympics."

My mouth dropped. "Wait, you're telling me you went to the Olympics?"

"I did."

"Holy shit. Did you win anything?"

"A bronze," he said nonchalantly.

"You won an Olympic bronze?" I repeated.

"I did," he said.

I was shocked to learn I was sitting next to a world-class athlete. "Wow. That's impressive."

"Thanks."

"Do you still compete?" I asked.

"Nope," he said and there was a hint of disgust in his voice. "I messed up my arm, and that was that. I realized my heart wasn't in it anymore either. I called it a day and moved on. I had a few sponsorships that afforded me the startup money I needed for my company. It doesn't take long for people to forget who you are. I would say my Olympic buzz faded about two years after I won the medal. It was nice to fade back into obscurity. I went back to my life. I should say, I actually started my life."

"I imagine there's a lot of training involved to prepare for something like that," I said.

He nodded again. "Pretty much a fulltime job. You have to eat right, work out all the time, and avoid alcohol. My teenage years were consumed by training. I'm just glad I rose hot and fast and fizzled by the age of twenty. I still had time to get on with my life."

"That is very cool," I said.

"What's your claim to fame?" he asked.

I scoffed. "My dad was the doctor for a bunch of Hollywood elites," I said.

"Did you meet any of the famous people that live in LA?" he asked.

I shrugged. "A few. I used to hang out at his office when I was younger. I met a few people, but they weren't anyone to me. Just another of Dad's patients."

"And your mom was a doctor?" he questioned.

"Yep. Dad was a cardiologist and Mom was a general practitioner."

"You were destined to be a doctor," he said.

"I guess you could say that."

"That's the second time you've made me think you are second guessing the doctor track," he said and refilled his glass.

"It isn't that I don't want to be a doctor," I said. "I do. I just sometimes wonder if I jumped into it too fast. I just always knew I was going to be a doctor and never considered anything else."

"Ah, the what if scenario," he said knowingly.

"Exactly. I'm out here fixing it. I'm going to go back, and my head will be straight. I'm going to tackle my work and go after the head of the department position."

He burst into laughter. "You just told me you were working too hard. Now you're going to go back home and work even harder?"

He was making a very valid point. I didn't want to talk about work anymore. I was supposed to be escaping all of that. "You know, when I came here, I planned on spending the bulk of my time naked," I laughed. "I was committed to living the life of a nudist."

"Yeah, I remember," he laughed. "You seemed to be off to a good start. Do you plan on stripping the moment I'm gone?"

"Maybe," I teased.

"Don't let me hold you back," he said with a wink. "Technically, I've already seen it."

"No way!" I laughed. "Not happening, buddy."

"Suit yourself, but I certainly haven't been holding back."

"I know," I blurted out before I could even think about what I was saying.

His eyes twinkled with mischief. "I know you know."

"You were doing it on purpose!"

"Nah, but if you were going to look, I wasn't going to stop you," he said nonchalantly. "I'm not ashamed. You're a doctor. Nudity shouldn't be a thing for you."

"It isn't but this is different," I argued.

"Is it?"

"Do you sleep naked?" I asked him.

"Yep," he nodded. "Most of the time. Why are you asking? Planning to unzip my bag in the middle of the night?"

"No," I said. "Maybe I'll sleep on the beach tonight and you can have the bed on your last night."

"And why would you do that?" he asked.

"I don't know," I shrugged. "It seems very freeing."

"You mean you want to sleep naked on the beach?" he teased.

"Not directly on the beach," I retorted. "I don't need sand in places sand should not be."

"There's a shower," he replied easily.

I held out my empty glass for him to refill. "I think I want to take a dip."

"A dip?"

I felt warm and knew it was the alcohol coursing through my system. "Yes, I want to go swimming. Look how calm the water is. It's so pretty."

"Do it," he encouraged.

"Are you going in?" I asked.

"Maybe."

I took a long, healthy drink from my glass. I wouldn't have been able to do that before the first glass to loosen things up. It didn't even burn anymore. I stood up and put my empty glass on the porch floor and stepped off the porch. I started my walk to the water and paused once to see if he was following. He was still sitting on the chair.

"Coming?" I asked in a sultry voice. I was playing with fire, and I didn't care.

I watched him finish his drink and stand up. He took off his shirt and dropped it on the chair before following me down the path. I stripped out of my tank and dropped it on the path before undoing the button of my little jean shorts. I stepped out of them and kept going. Then I lost the bra, tossing it onto the sand before walking towards the water. Next, it was my panties. I walked straight into the water without looking back.

I walked out to my knees and then dove under. The water was cool, but not cold as it washed over me. I had never felt more alive in my life than I did in that moment. There was nothing but me, the moonlight and a huge ocean. Oh, and the hot guy who was probably standing on the beach watching me. I didn't even care that he'd seen me naked again.

I came up for air just in time to see him dive under. When he resurfaced, he was smiling like an idiot. Hell, his smile was probably a mirror image of my own. "Feel better?" he asked as he slowly cut through the water towards me.

The waves rocked me, gently lifting and dropping me down once again. "I feel a million percent better," I told him.

"Me too," he grinned. "But I've been doing this every night."

"I know."

"You're missing out if you don't do this after I'm gone," he said. "Don't be shy. You're one with the earth out here. You can be naked, and no one is going to know."

"You'll know," I reminded him.

"And I'll be praising the heavens for putting such a beautiful creature on this planet," he said in a husky voice.

I stared at him for half a beat before diving back into the water. I swam out a little deeper. I was comfortable swimming in the ocean. I'd been doing it all my life. I knew the power of the sea and respected it. Right now, we were safe, and I wasn't going to worry about anything except feeling the moment.

I felt his hand brush over my calf and knew he was following me into the deeper water. I laughed and spun around only to find myself spinning directly into his arms. I stared into his eyes. Then he was kissing me. My arms wrapped around him as he deepened the kiss. The water threatened to knock me over. His arms wrapped around my waist and pulled me against his hard chest. I felt him moving me through the water. He stopped when we were about thigh-deep in the water.

He stopped kissing me and looked down into my eyes. "Was that okay?" he whispered.

I answered by kissing him back. Then I was wrapping my legs around his waist. He kissed me to the point I was dizzy. I couldn't let go of the man. My hands snaked up his back and into that thick, black hair before running both hands down his cheeks. The man was solid muscle. Everywhere I touched him it was nothing but strength and power. I had never dated a man like him. I thought I preferred my men to be lean. Boy, had I been missing out.

He pulled his mouth from mine. His chest was heaving up and down, my nipples scraping over his hard pectoral muscles. "I have to stop," he breathed.

I was disappointed, but it was probably the right thing to do. "Okay."

"I don't want to," he quickly added. "That's why I have to."

"You don't want to?" I murmured.

His hand reached up and pushed my hair back from my face. "Definitely not. I have to stop now, or I won't be able to."

I smiled at him and appreciated the compliment. "I don't want you to stop."

"You're sure?" he asked with his muscles tense against me. I could feel his erection just as strong and powerful as the rest of him. I moved my hips a few inches and pulled a groan from him.

"I'm very sure."

"I don't have a condom," he said. "I thought I was coming out to a deserted island."

He was making a very good point and the rational side of me should have followed his lead. "I'm on the pill and I can assure you I'm very clean and healthy."

He grinned and kissed the tip of my nose. "I'm going to tell you a secret, but you cannot use this against me later."

"What's that?"

"I've been celibate for so long I can't even remember how long it's been," he said in a low voice. "You're not catching anything from me."

I stared at him and ran through a list of reasons why I should stop this right where it was. None of the reasons held any water. I didn't give a shit. I wanted the man, and this was my last chance to have him. I had never had a one-night stand and it felt about damn time that I did.

"Why don't we go back to the cottage?" I whispered.

He kissed me in response. His tongue swept inside my mouth. His arms tightened around me, and we started to move. I wrapped my legs around his waist and tried to get closer to him. I was on fire. Now that I'd given myself permission, I couldn't seem to shut it down. I was crazy with need. My body was liquid fire as I rubbed my pussy against his erection.

"Fuck this," he growled, and the next thing I knew, I was being lowered to the beach.

As it turned out, we weren't making it to the cottage, which was perfectly okay with me.

Chapter Sixteen

Jake

The woman was too much for my very limited self-control. When she wrapped her legs around me, I was a goner. I had to fight to keep myself from completely losing control and pounding inside her. This was a woman who needed to be treated with care. She needed a gentle hand. I propped myself up on my elbows to keep from squishing her. She probably weighed half of what I did. "Are you okay?" I asked with a shaky breath.

"I will be," she smiled and reached up to caress a hand over my cheek.

"I have to be honest with you, it's been a while and—" I stopped. I didn't want to get into the story of my ex-wife. I'd had sex with exactly one person after Amanda. Fifteen years of doing the same thing with the same woman left me at a disadvantage. I didn't remember how to just do it.

"Good," she smiled. "For me as well."

"Things are a little different than they used to be," I said even as I fought the urges rocking through my body. All her hot, silky skin was rubbing against me. The water made us both slick and that very basic male instinct was clawing at my insides to come out and play.

"Don't ask," she said in a harsh tone. "Don't make this weird."

"I don't want to piss you off, hurt you, or offend you," I said, and dropped a soft kiss on her forehead. "I'm dying right now. My body is primed and ready to explode. I'm trying to restrain myself."

She reached around and grabbed a hard handful of my ass and squeezed. Her nails dug into my flesh as she lifted her head. "Don't treat me like I'm a fragile flower. We're on an island all by ourselves. We're in the wild. Let's really be in the wild."

I didn't want to get my hopes up, but it sounded like she was giving me carte blanche. "You're sure?"

She slapped at my shoulder. "Stop questioning this! Fuck me!"

I slammed my mouth over hers and kissed her so hard I actually worried I had cut my lip on her teeth. I gave into the instinct screaming at me to be let free. My mouth moved over her neck. I could taste the salt water on her flesh as I trailed my mouth down to her breasts. Her hands were running through my hair. Her chest heaved up and down as she gasped and groaned with every lap of my tongue over her nipples.

I rolled to my side and kissed her again with my hand caressing the breasts I had just loved with my mouth. Her back arched, pushing her full breasts into my palm. I massaged them, tweaking the nipples before sliding my hand down her flat stomach and between her legs.

"I've thought about this from the very moment I saw you," I whispered against her lips.

"Me too."

"You wanted me?" I asked with a smile before kissing her again.

"I thought about it. I might have dreamed about it."

That made me hot. "You dreamed about fucking me?" I asked in a gruff voice.

"Maybe," she teased.

"Did you dream about this?" I asked, and pushed a finger inside her.

She gasped and arched her back again. "Yes," she groaned. "More."

"More?" I whispered before kissing her again.

She moaned in response. I pushed in a second finger. Her sweet little moans and soft whimpers fueled me to keep going. She reached up and scratched at my arm as she writhed against the sand. "Don't stop," she begged.

I sucked her erect nipple into my mouth. Her back arched again. I sucked harder while pushing my fingers in deeper. She groaned and pulled at my hair. It was the first indication that she might be just a little wild. I would have loved to pursue that track but not the first time, and not with a woman who had hated me a few days ago. I was too far gone to walk away from this woman. I had to be inside her, but not until she got her release. I could be a generous lover, given the opportunity.

I kept going until she cried out as her orgasm broke free. I immediately moved over her and lined up the head of my cock to push inside her. My breath caught in my throat. She'd gone completely still and was staring up at me. Her hands rubbed down my arms.

"Ready?" I asked.

"Stop talking and just do it," she groaned.

I pushed in. My cock slid deep with no resistance. The moment I was fully seated inside her, her sweet pussy clamped down around me. I groaned and drew my head back to process the millions of feelings coursing through my body. I had to fight the urge to explode deep inside her. I could not be a minute man.

"I can't move," I breathed.

"Move," she demanded.

"I can't. I'm so close."

"Take me, Jake," she murmured and put her hand on the back of my neck and pulled my face to hers. She kissed me with just enough passion to send me soaring. I broke our mouths free of each other and pushed off her with my cock still firmly buried inside her.

"I'd say hold on, but I think you're out of luck," I growled.

I started slow until I found my rhythm. Then I gave into the wildfire spreading through my veins. Her sounds of pleasure washed around me. Water tickled my toes as the waves came in. Nothing was going to stop me from reaching the point of ecstasy. I moved harder and faster until I was nearly blinded with the pleasure pumping through my veins. I thrust once again, and it took me over the edge. Her shouts told me she was falling right along with me. The feeling was euphoric. There was a ringing in my ears as my hips rocked and jerked of their own volition.

I was helpless to combat what was happening to my body. It had been so long since I'd found that kind of pleasure. My body seemed unsure how to process it all.

I lowered myself over her and kissed her once again. "Good?" I asked.

"Are you asking me to grade your performance?" she laughed.

"No. I can feel how well I did. I just wanted to make sure you were okay. You were screaming pretty loud there."

I was teasing her. She slapped at my shoulder. "Stop."

"I heard you," I said and kissed her. "I felt you. I can feel how wet you are."

"You weren't exactly quiet," she reminded me.

"Nope, and I wasn't trying to be," I said with a laugh. "Who's going to hear us? We could have screamed at the top of our lungs."

Her arms slid around my neck and pulled me close. "I was pretty close."

Just then, a wave came in and reached all the way to her waist. She yelped at the same time as I jumped to my feet. I reached down and helped her up. "I'm full of sand," she complained.

"There's the outdoor shower," I said. "I'll make sure to rinse you. All of you. Every nook and cranny."

She giggled as I took her hand and led her up to the outdoor shower that was mounted on a small cement slab. I pulled the cord and ran my hand down her back and over her ass. I rinsed the sand away before washing my feet and knees. I shut off the water and realized it was over. This was like the end of a first date. Did I walk her to the cottage and then go back to my sleeping bag on the beach? Did I kiss her? I wasn't sure what the rules were with this particular situation.

"Stay with me," she said softly.

"You're sure?" I asked.

She took my hand and led me up the path, walking past the discarded clothing on the way. The path was lit with faint solar lights that did little to illuminate anything more than just the ground. We made it to the cottage, and she pushed open the door. Once we were inside, she closed and locked the door, which I found kind of silly considering the only two people on the island were behind the locked door.

"I guess we're sleeping in the buff," I said with a laugh when she tossed a towel at me.

"I prefer it that way, don't you?" she asked with a flirty smile.

"Absolutely, especially if there's a naked body next to mine."

"Just any naked body?" she teased.

"I prefer the other naked body to be just a little curvier and softer than mine is," I replied before pulling the quilt back. It was going to be good to sleep in a bed again. I loved the beach, but I wasn't exactly a teen anymore. My back was a little sore from sleeping on the sand.

She climbed in, and much to my pleasure, she scooted close to me. I didn't want to keep comparing her to Amanda, but this was nice. Amanda hated snuggling and she refused to sleep naked with me. There was a certain intimacy to being skin to skin with someone. It completed the whole ritual. First, I was inside her and now I was beside her.

"What time do you think he'll be by tomorrow?" she asked softly.

"I don't know," I said. "Afternoon or late morning I would assume. I guess it all depends on what he's got going on for the day."

"I hope we get to sleep in," she murmured.

"Me too," I said, and squeezed her a little tighter.

I closed my eyes and held her. This was definitely not on the agenda, but I was so glad it had happened. It had been way too long since I had held a woman's soft body against mine. Too long since I listened to the soft breathing of a woman lulled into a state of contentment after sex. Way back in the beginning, Amanda and I had been close. I missed sharing myself with someone. I missed being the other half to someone special.

When I went home tomorrow, I was going to change things. I was going to put myself out there and start dating. It was time I moved on. I didn't want to be alone. I had taken the necessary time off from the world of relationships and now I felt ready to wade back into the dating pool. There had to be someone out there for me. Someone who would be loyal and supportive.

Gabby certainly felt right, but I knew this was not going to happen again. I would leave tomorrow, and I doubted I would ever see her again. All I could do was quietly thank her for ripping the band-aid off and getting me back on track to living again.

"Goodnight," she whispered into the dark.

"Goodnight."

"Does it feel better to be in here with me or out on the beach?" she asked.

I chuckled softly. "That's an easy answer—you. I would always choose this over a sandy beach."

She patted my chest. "Good answer."

I thought about asking her if she'd like to go for round two. I was ready. If I was only going to be with her this one night, it seemed like a good idea to make the most of it. Unfortunately, my cock was ready and willing, but my brain was exhausted. I could already feel the sleep trying to pull me under. I tried to fight it, but with the limited sleep I'd been getting on the beach and the strong scotch pumping through my blood, I was no match.

I fell asleep with her in my arms and hoped I would wake the following morning early enough to take advantage of her generous spirit one last time before I had to leave.

Chapter Seventeen

Gabby

I woke with a start. The first thing that hit my conscious mind was the fact there was a body next to mine. There was so much hot skin touching mine. I pulled back a few inches and opened my eyes. Then it all came rushing back to me. Jake. We had sex last night and slept together. A slow smile spread over my lips. I leaned forward and was about to kiss him when I realized it was daylight. Like, super bright daylight. There was a faint noise in the distance. It stood out because it had been so quiet for the last week. The occasional boat would pass in the distance, but none ever came close to the island. The only other noise we heard was the occasional jet flying overhead. I had grown used to the silence and was not thrilled with the noise.

"Oh, shit!" I said and slapped at his chest. "Jake! I hear the boat. Oleg's coming!"

He stirred and then groaned. "What?"

"Oleg!" I said and jumped out of bed. "Get up!"

"Oh, shit," he said, and threw the blankets off.

"You're naked!" I shrieked.

"So, are you," he shot back.

"Oh no," I groaned. "Your clothes. My clothes. They're strewn all over. He's going to know."

"Relax," he said. "My suitcase is still in here, right?"

"Yes," I nodded. "Out there. Hurry!"

While he walked out of the room, I pulled open the drawers, pulled on a pair of panties, and found some shorts that were mostly clean. I didn't bother with a bra. I pulled on a hoodie and quickly tried to finger comb my hair. I stepped in front of the mirror and cringed. I had sex hair. It was wild and sticking up in every direction. I looked a hot mess.

There was nothing I could do but put it up in a messy bun. "Are you dressed yet?" I called out.

He didn't answer. I walked into the living room to find him standing at the door wearing just a pair of shorts. "What are you doing?" I asked. "Get dressed!"

"I don't think that's going to be necessary."

"What are you talking about?" I said.

He bent down and picked something up before turning to look at me. "This," he said.

I stared at the small Igloo. "What's that?" I asked the obvious. It was somewhat of a rhetorical question.

"It's a cooler," he said. "And there's a box of groceries."

I could feel the blood rushing from my face. "Groceries?" I squeaked.

"Oleg has already come and gone."

"No!" I shrieked. "Go after him. He can't be far. I heard the boat."

"I'm not going to chase after a fucking boat," he growled.

I stared at him. His hair was sticking up in several different directions. If the situation wasn't so dire, I would definitely want to jump his bones again. But that was not what this was about. "I'll go," I said.

"Go where?" he asked as I rushed past him with no shoes on.

I ran down the path towards the dock. "Oleg!" I cried out as I ran onto the dock.

I could see a faint dot in the distance and just knew that was him. He wasn't stopping. I jumped up and down and waved my hands in the air. He was long gone. If history predicted the future, Oleg was not coming back until the next week grocery delivery.

I dropped my chin to my chest. This was my fault. I should have known better. Last night, I thought I could live footloose and fancy free. Now I was stuck with him for another week. It wasn't that I disliked the guy,

I just didn't want to live with him. I was supposed to be here alone for a month. I was supposed to get to be alone with just my thoughts.

"Gabby?" I heard Jake say.

I spun around to look at him. "He's gone," I said, and threw my hands up. "He's long gone."

He was still shirtless and shoeless. He shoved his hands in his pockets and looked around. "We'll figure it out," he said.

I glared at him. "Figure it out?" I hissed. "You did this on purpose."

"Did what?" he asked with a confused expression.

"You got me drunk last night and crawled into bed with me knowing I would sleep like the dead. You purposely slept right through his arrival. You did this on purpose!"

"That's ridiculous," he said, and actually laughed.

"I'm not laughing, Jake! How could you do this?"

"Oh shit, you're serious right now," he said, and the smile fell away.

"Yes, I'm serious," I snapped. "This is not funny. This is a disaster."

"I know you aren't actually blaming me for this," he said.

"You got me drunk."

"You weren't drunk," he shot back.

"I wasn't completely sober."

"Are you saying I took advantage of you?" he asked in a low growl.

I realized I might have been a little hasty and accusatory. "Not like that, but you got me drunk in order to soften me up."

"The hell I did," he growled. "I offered you a drink. The rest happened because we both wanted it."

"Why did you offer me that scotch?" I asked.

He shook his head. "You really are a piece of work. Heaven forbid anyone ever offers you a drink. You know, for the record, last night happened because we wanted it. I wasn't drunk, and I know you weren't. We drank. Period. You're the one who invited me to stay in your bed. But trust me, that isn't going to happen again. We're going to be here for another week. Trust me, I'll keep my distance."

He turned to walk away. "Wait!" I called out.

"Done, Gabby. Done."

"We need to talk about this," I said.

"No, we don't," he said and kept walking.

I trailed behind him. "What are you going to do?"

"I'm going to get my fishing gear and go fishing," he said.

"And then what?"

"Are you my cruise director?" he said snidely.

"I mean, when are we going to talk?" I said and managed to catch up to him.

"We're not," he said. "Why would we talk? You're pissed at me... again. You're going to tell me to stay out of your way and that it's your cottage. Blah, blah, blah. I've heard it before. Trust me, I don't want to be in your cottage or anywhere near you."

"What the hell," I gasped. "You're treating me like a one-night stand."

"Newsflash, Gabby, you are," he shot back.

"I am not."

He stopped walking and turned around to look at me. "Are you suggesting we have sex again?" he asked.

"No!"

"Then technically, it was a one-nighter. Now, if you'll excuse me, I have a date with a fishing pole. We had sex. Get over it. Don't make a big deal out of it. We've got another week together. I plan on enjoying that week. We managed the last week. I'll sleep in the hammock or on the beach. I'll use the kitchen when I need to and shower when I need to. Other than that, we don't have to see each other. We definitely don't have to talk to each other. You do you. I'll worry about me."

He stormed away and this time, I didn't chase him. This was why I didn't have sex with strangers. Not that I had a lot of sex in general, but the few times I did, it never ended well. I hated the feeling of sharing my body with someone and then never talking to them again. It felt weird. It felt icky.

This was all my fault. He had given me plenty of outs and I shut him down. I could blame him, but this was just as much my fault. Not that I was ever going to tell him that. I wasn't sure where he was going to be, and I didn't want to have another encounter with him. I went back to the beach and picked up my discarded clothing. When I got back to the cottage, he wasn't around.

I settled in with a book after cleaning up a bit. It was strange to be on the island with him, but not around him. I could practically feel his presence. I hoped he would stay away. I didn't think I could handle being near him and not want him. Even when I was so furious with him this morning, I still wanted the man.

I read until I realized I was reading just to read and nothing was sinking in. I tossed the book to the side and went to bed. I was tired, but I couldn't fall asleep. I stared up at the sky and wondered where he was. Was he ten feet away in the hammock or out on the beach? I shook it off. It didn't matter where he was. We were not friends. We were nothing more than two people who had sex one time.

Really good sex. But that didn't matter. I could have more sex when I got back to LA. I was definitely going to do that. It'd been a while, but I didn't remember sex being that good. I wanted to see if it was just him, or if I had unlocked something inside me that allowed me to finally have the kind of sex that I heard other people talking about.

I was dead asleep and in the throes of a very wild erotic dream when I heard something loud. I opened my eyes and stared around the room. It was very dark. The glow from the numbers on the digital clock I had turned towards the wall cast an eerie red glow over the room. I couldn't figure out what had woken me.

I realized then it was another storm. This one sounded much worse than the first. I could hear the wind howling. The noise I heard was the rain slamming against the window. "Holy cow," I whispered, and jumped out of bed.

I tried to look outside but I couldn't see much of anything. I walked into the living room. I had left the window open. I moved to close the window and slipped on the wet floor. "Dammit," I muttered and picked myself up so I could close the window.

My curiosity got the best of me. I had to see just how bad it was outside. I wasn't a total evil bitch. If Jake was out there, he could be in real danger. I pulled open the door and gasped. The trees were practically bent in half. The rain was coming down from every which way. This wasn't good. The poor man had to be in a bad way.

I stepped onto the porch with rain slamming against my bare legs. My hair was blowing everywhere. I walked to the edge of the porch to look into the darkness. I was assuming he was in the hammock. I hoped he was. I couldn't imagine him out there on the beach in this mess. Sand was blowing and hitting me in the face and sticking to my teeth and skin.

I could see the blue tarp snapping in the wind. I managed to get a glimpse of the hammock swaying hard in the wind. There was no way he could sleep out in this weather. Why hadn't he knocked on the door? He knew he could come inside. He couldn't actually think I was that horrible. There was no way he was going to hear me.

I went back inside to get my shoes so I could get his attention. I was actually very concerned for his safety. No matter what was or wasn't happening between us, I didn't wish death on anyone. He was a good guy. He just wasn't my guy.

Chapter Eighteen

Jake

This was miserable. I was hardcore, but this was just stupid. The hammock was actually making me a little seasick. It was rocking so hard I was afraid it was going to dump me on the ground. If the hammock didn't drop me, the trees were going to snap. This was one hell of a storm, but I refused to admit defeat. She wanted my ass outside. I was determined to stay out. She could have that damn cottage with the roof over her head. She could stay dry.

I pulled my sleeping bag a little tighter around me. It wasn't cold, but it was wet and windy, which made it feel cold. A gust came up, blowing the hammock so hard I had to reach up and hold the edge to avoid getting dumped. I had so much sand in my teeth and eyes I could probably build a sandcastle. The tarp was ineffective. There was no way to keep the rain out. My sleeping bag was repelling the water now, but it wouldn't last forever. Soon, I was going to be waterlogged.

"Such bullshit," I muttered.

Every minute I sat out in the rain, the more pissed I got. After listening to her ridiculous tirade, I had gone fishing and caught nothing, which pissed me off even more. The entire day had been a series of irritating events. All of it stemmed from the incident this morning. I couldn't believe she had the audacity to blame me for her sleeping through Oleg's arrival. We had both had a few drinks. She was the one who invited me into bed. I would have been satisfied sleeping on the beach.

I wondered why Oleg dumped the groceries and ran. At least, I had wondered that until I walked the path to the cottage and found my underwear. The man probably saw the discarded clothing and put two and two together. Unfortunately, two and two did not always equal four. In this case, it had been a five. Now, I was stuck on this damn island for another week with a woman that drove me crazy. She was batshit crazy. I wanted nothing to do with her. I had enough of women pushing me to the very limits of my patience.

There was no way I was going to sit around and let another woman punish me for basically existing. Amanda always made me feel like I was two inches tall. Somehow, everything we ever fought about was my fault. If I couldn't make one of her fancy dinners because I was working, she wouldn't talk to me for a week. It became a cycle. I would screw up and the only way she would talk to me again was if I bought her jewelry. There was always a reason. I was so sick of the games.

A hurricane was just about the right way to end this day. Even Mother Nature had a vendetta against me. One had to really do some serious self-reflection when it seemed like every female he encountered had a problem with him. "It's not you, it's me," I muttered.

"Jake!" I thought I heard my name.

I shook it off. The wind could screw with my hearing. I had been hearing all kinds of weird things. I pulled the sleeping bag up and tried to shave off a few inches of my height to sink deeper into the bag. This was one of the downsides to being tall.

"Jake!" I heard my name again. This time, I was certain it wasn't just the wind.

I struggled to sit up and peer around the edge of the tarp. It was Gabby standing under the safety of the covered porch. She waved at me. "Jake!" she called out.

I rolled my eyes and laid back in the hammock. Fuck her. She didn't want me anywhere near her precious body or in the cottage she declared was hers. Even now, she had relegated me outside while she hid under the covered porch. Even dogs got better treatment. The woman was cold and ruthless. She was probably just trying to gauge my misery.

Fuck her. Fuck her cruelty. I refused to give her the satisfaction of seeing just how miserable I was.

The one good thing about the storm was the idea that it might bring Oleg back a little earlier. Maybe he'd come out and check on us tomorrow. If he did, I would absolutely jump in his boat and beg him to get me the hell off the island. She'd probably push me into the boat or make me hold the damn anchor. I closed my eyes and tried to go to sleep. The sooner I went to sleep, the sooner I could wake up and be done with this nightmare.

"Jake!"

I jerked and nearly fell out of the hammock once again. I popped my head out of the bag. "What?" I snapped.

She was standing beside me with a jacket over her head, as if that was going to do any good. The rain was coming up and from the side. "Come inside!" she shouted over the sound of the howling wind.

I heard a tree branch crack. "No."

"Jake, this is stupid! Get your ass inside."

"No!" I shouted again.

"Stop acting like a child! You're going to get killed out here."

"And that would be my fault too, wouldn't it?" I snarled.

"Would you just get inside?" she asked again. "I'm offering you somewhere warm, safe, and dry."

"Offering me?" I snapped. "Gee, your grace, will I also be expected to lick your boots? Bow?"

"Stop it!"

"No thanks," I said. "Go away."

"Stop this!" she shrieked and actually stomped her foot. "I'm not going to stand out here and argue with you about your own damn safety. You're being an idiot. Get your ass inside."

"Sorry, I'm not a glutton for punishment. You'll probably blame this storm on me too. Think I conjured it up so I could get inside *your* cottage and put the moves on you."

"Whatever," she growled. "Keep your dumbass out here. I hope you drown."

"I'm sure you do."

"I'm sorry," she said. "I didn't mean that, but you are acting like an idiot, and you are bound to get hurt or killed out here."

"Get out of here!" I shouted.

She spun around and walked away. I wanted to go inside. I wasn't trying to get killed on vacation, but to go in would admit defeat. I didn't want to give her the satisfaction of being right. I would get blown out of the damn hammock before I tucked tail and walked into that cottage. It would be at least another hour before I had to call uncle, but the storm was kicking my ass. This was only proving her point that I was being childish. I could expect her snide look. She'd walk around the cottage like she was king shit. She was right and I was wrong.

I rolled out of the hammock and hit the ground. I was barefoot as I walked around the cottage and up to the front porch. "Are you fucking kidding me?" I growled.

My suitcase with all my dry clothes was sitting on the porch. I had left it there earlier to keep it out of the sand and dry in case it did rain. Now, it was thoroughly soaked. The porch was wet. Everything was wet. I was wet, and the clothes I had on were drenched.

I expected the door to be locked. When I reached for the handle and turned it, I was surprised to find it unlocked. Surprised and irritated. She was going to rub that in my face as well. She knew I was going to give in and come inside eventually. I stepped into the cottage and found her sitting on the couch with a cup of hot chocolate in her hand.

She gave me a look that just about had me walking into the ocean. "What?" I snapped.

"You're soaked."

"No shit, Sherlock," I hissed. "Newsflash, it's raining outside."

"I thought the tarp kept you dry," she said nonchalantly.

"You know what else keeps me dry?" I asked in a syrupy sweet voice.

"What?"

"The cottage I fucking paid for!" I growled.

"I told you to come in," she argued.

"Yes, you did, three hours into the storm," I said. "But you forgot to tell me to sit and stay. I would hate to disobey the master of the island. I mean, it is yours after all. You're the queen of the castle. I'm just the lowly peasant that fucked you silly last night and then ruined your life. Oh, and let's not forget I also forced you to get drunk. My crimes are endless."

"You're dripping water on the floor," she said.

"Yes, that's what happens when you get caught in a hurricane with no shelter!" I snapped. "Thanks for leaving my bag on the porch. Now I have nothing dry."

"I didn't put your shit on the porch," she said. "You did."

"You saw the rain. You knew my shit was out there. I'm sure the door was locked, which would keep me from putting inside. You could have at least had the common decency to put it inside."

"Oh, so that's my fault," she said with a laugh.

"Just like me missing the boat with Oleg is my fault," I shot back. "I'm going to dry off. You might want to avert your eyes. I've got nothing dry. I'm not putting wet clothes back on."

"I'll see if I have something for you to put on," she said.

I gave her a dry look and then made a point to stare at her body and then mine. "Yeah, I'm sure that'll work.

"I have some basketball shorts that are actually really big," she said.

"Yeah, my balls can't be bunched up like that," I told her. "No thanks. I'll sleep naked."

"No!"

I closed my eyes and begged for patience. "You need to take a big fucking step back," I said. "I'm so done taking orders from you. You are not the queen. You are not the boss of me!"

I knew how stupid and ridiculous that sounded. I couldn't help it. She had an uncanny knack for pushing my buttons. I stomped out of the room and into the bathroom. I slammed the door and grabbed one of the four towels to dry off. I stripped out of the wet clothes and hung them over the shower rod. I dried off the best I could.

"Jake?" Gabby called out.

"What?" I snapped.

"I brought you a shirt and shorts," she said.

She wanted to play this game; I was down for it. I opened the bathroom door in all my naked glory. The look on her face was absolutely priceless. "Here." She thrust a shirt and shorts at me.

"Gabby, get real," I said. "I'm not wearing your shit."

"Well it's better than being naked," she said.

I looked at her and grinned before dropping the towel on the floor. "Weird, because you said almost the exact opposite last night. If you'll excuse me, I'm going to pour myself a glass of my scotch, assuming you didn't drink it all or pour it out."

"Of course, I didn't," she said defiantly.

"Good. And no, you can't have any."

"Jake—"

"If you'll excuse me," I said, and brushed my naked body past hers.

"You can't just sit on the couch naked!" she protested.

"Watch me, if you'd like," I called out and went for the bottle that was still sitting on the counter. "But no matter how pretty you beg, I'm not fucking you again."

It was crass and I would normally never speak so crudely, but I had no more fucks to give. I grabbed a cup and poured myself two fingers of scotch. I was glad we hadn't finished the bottle last night. I heard her footsteps behind me but I kept my back to her.

"Still not wearing your shit," I said.

"I brought you a blanket," she said. "Unless you plan on airing things out."

I smirked and took another drink. "Trust me, I'm good. Thanks for the blanket. Very magnanimous of you."

"Look, I didn't mean to blame you earlier," I said. "I was just pissed."

"Yep, I figured that one out all on my own. Believe it or not, I'm not as dumb as I look."

"I never said you were dumb," she said.

"Unless you have something of value I want to hear, I would suggest you go hide in your bedroom," I said. "I'm not hiding myself from you." I turned around and looked her dead in the eye. I dared her to say something about my nudity. I took a slow drink from the glass. Her cheeks were red as she stormed down the hall. I laughed when I heard the bedroom door slam.

"Score one for me," I muttered.

The win wasn't anything to celebrate considering I was naked and standing in the living room. But I would take the wins where I could get them.

Chapter Nineteen

Gabby

I sat on the edge of my bed and listened to the weather howling outside. I should just go to sleep. Unfortunately, I couldn't sleep. He was out there completely naked. How in the hell was I supposed to sleep with that happening? I wanted nothing to do with him. We were fire and ice. He was so damn sexy and stubborn.

Even the way we argued was hot. He made me want to strangle him and kiss him at the same time. I had never met anyone so damn infuriating. I liked to think I was pretty easy going. High-strung, but still easy going when it came to people. I didn't let them bother me. I dealt with so much crazy stuff all day every day, I couldn't let a few insults get to me. It was the suit of armor I wore to keep myself safe from people and their feelings. People could be very emotional. I used to describe it to my friend as watching Hallmark movies all day, but rarely did those movies have a happy ending. It was a constant assault on the emotions. I would be severely dehydrated if I let myself cry all day.

I climbed under the covers and tried to force myself to go to sleep. The storm would be over by morning, and he would be gone. He'd go back to his section of beach, and I could just do what I did all day, which was a lot of nothing. I wasn't going to admit I was a little bored. It would have been nice to hang out with him. Unfortunately, I burned that bridge. Hell, I blew that bridge to smithereens.

I pulled the pillow over my face and tried to count sheep. I started going through the things I was going to do when I got home. No matter how much I mentally distanced myself from the naked man on my couch, it kept coming back to him. I couldn't stop picturing him naked in the kitchen. His body was forever imprinted on my brain. He would have made a hell of a pinup. I wondered why he was single. I knew he wasn't gay. He was sexy, successful, and despite how much he irritated me, he was charming.

If I met him in the real world, I would be attracted to him. I knew my dad would like him. Although my dad was all about me marrying and settling down with a nice doctor or maybe a lawyer, I knew my dad would have liked Jake. He had that downhome thing that appealed to my dad. If he were alive, he would tell me to quit being so damn mean to the man and go out with him.

My dad had warned me I was going to end up very alone in my later years if I didn't cool my jets. Those were his words. He was always telling me to cool my jets. Yet, he was also the man who pushed and encouraged me to work harder. I had a tendency to be dismissive of people that tried to get into my personal orbit.

I closed my eyes and went to that place in my mind that I could talk to my parents. It usually ended up just being Dad I talked to. Mom had been gone for ten years. It was sad to admit, but I barely remembered what her voice sounded like. I couldn't quite conjure up her image. Not like I could with my dad.

It's me, Dad. I miss you. This last month has been so hard. I thought I would be okay. I went right back to work after your funeral. I didn't tell anyone where I'd been for the weekend. I couldn't bring myself to actually say the words. Now I'm here on this island and I'm just making a real mess of things.

"Ah, my sweet Gabriel," I could hear him say. "You are such a strong girl. I blame myself for teaching you to push through all the things that make us human."

"I'm not strong, Dad. I'm on autopilot. I don't know what I'm doing. You always told me I should focus on my work. I've done that. I always do that. What if I'm doing it all wrong? I don't want to be alone for the rest of my

life but every time someone even thinks about getting close to me, I push them away."

I could hear his soft laughter bouncing in my mind. "Gabby, you're still young. You're going to have a full life with a family and friends. You just have to find the balance."

"It took you and Mom a long time to find that balance," I told him in my mind. "You guys were almost forty when you decided to start a family."

"Your mom and I wanted to make sure we were established and could give you everything you would want and need," he explained in that way he always did. "We used to talk about having more kids, but it just wasn't in the cards. One of our biggest regrets was not having you sooner. Don't make that same mistake. It's okay to love. It's okay to be loved."

"But what if I get hurt?"

"You probably will get hurt," he said. "That's part of living. We've always tried give you plenty of room to grow and explore. I think we should have done a better job teaching you how to love."

I almost laughed. "I don't think you have to be taught to love. Most people don't, but apparently, I do. I just don't know how to let down my guard. I can't lose anyone else."

"Gabby, you didn't lose us. We're here with you. We're always here. Let yourself love. Be loved."

"How do I know what love is?" I asked.

"You know," he assured me. His voice in my head grew faint. "Go easy on yourself. Let yourself love."

I sighed, feeling a little better after having the pseudo-conversation with my late father. If I ever saw a shrink, I'd probably be committed if I admitted to talking to dead people. I had work friends, but I had no one truly close to me. My father was all I had. I was going to try and take his advice. I wasn't going to pretend Jake was my destiny, but he was a practice run. This very strange relationship I had with him was opening new doors that had been previously closed. It was making me think about things I never imagined I would be considering. I was thinking about love and babies and all the other things.

When I finally fell asleep, it wasn't at all restful. I tossed and turned and thought about everything, but mostly him. We were stuck on the island for another week. I could make the best of it and choose to get along with him, or keep fighting what was happening. Then again, he wasn't exactly leaning towards being my best friend.

When I woke the next morning, I felt unsettled. Nothing felt right. It wasn't just the weather that was out of sorts. I got out of bed and walked to the window. "Dammit."

It was still raining, and the wind was still blowing. That did not bode well for the day. We were going to be trapped in this stupid cottage together. It was like putting two feral animals in the same cage and hoping they got along. I couldn't kick him out of the cottage. Not with weather like this. That meant I was likely going to be stuck in the bedroom while he took the rest of the house.

I walked to the bedroom door and very slowly opened it. If he was still sleeping, I didn't want to wake him. I was hoping to sneak into the kitchen and grab something to drink and maybe some food before I retreated to the bedroom once again. I needed to shower. I was hoping to get in and out before he rose. The house was dark with the clouds blocking the sun. I tiptoed down the short hall and looked towards the living room to see if he was still inside.

My breath caught. He was on the couch with the blanket half on the floor. One leg was over the back of the couch with the other stretched out and resting on the armrest. His nudity was on full display. I immediately averted my eyes. Almost immediately. It was hard not to look at such a beautiful specimen of the male body. He was tanner than he had been when he first got to the island last week. His hair looked wild, but his expression was one of peace.

I looked away but it was too late. His eyes popped open and stared directly at me. "Yes?" he asked in a gruff voice.

"I was just getting a drink," I said and quickly went into the kitchen.

I grabbed a bottle of water and a box of crackers, which wasn't exactly what I had been going for, but he flustered me. When I turned around again, he was just getting off the couch. He tossed the blanket to the couch and stared at me. "Problem?" he asked.

I had told myself I was going to be nice, but damn if he didn't bring out the worst in me. "Just wondering if you plan on spending the rest of the week naked."

"I might," he said. "Aren't you the one who wanted to be a nudist?"

"When I was alone."

"You've seen me naked," he said. "Shouldn't you be used to this by now?"

"I just don't understand why you feel the need to be naked all the time," I spat.

"I'm not naked all the time," he said. "I don't want to wear wet cloths. I'll chafe."

I rolled my eyes. "Whatever. It's still raining out, so I assume you'll be hanging out in here today."

"I might."

"I'll stick to the bedroom and stay out of your way," I said. "I'm going to take a quick shower, then you won't see me again."

"Good," he said, and started walking towards me.

I panicked and froze. I couldn't move. He walked right up to me and brushed his body in front of mine before moving down the hall. I hated it, but I watched him walk away. He walked into the bathroom and closed the door.

"What are you doing?" I frowned as I walked to the bathroom door.

"I'm taking a shower," he called through the door. "I got chilled last night. I need to warm up."

"I just told you I was going to get in the shower!"

"Too bad," he said.

"That's so rude!" I shrieked. "If we're going to live together, you have to be polite."

"That's good advice," he said. "You should take it."

"Why would you do that?" I growled and slapped my hand against the door. "I wanted to take a shower and then you could have the whole place to yourself."

"I'm already in here," he said with a laugh. "You snooze, you lose."

"You jerk!" I growled.

"Why don't you go outside and take a shower in the rain?" he teased. "You made me do it. Try a little of your own medicine. Lucky for you, it's a little warmer."

I slapped the door again. "I didn't make you do anything!"

Arguing through a closed door felt very futile. It wasn't getting me anywhere. He just pissed me off so much. I could walk away and go to the room. I didn't have to shower right this very minute. It was the principal of the matter. He heard me say I was going to shower, and he pushed his way inside. It was so damn rude. Every time I thought we could possibly be friends, he did something like this. He was insufferable.

"Go away," he said. "Let me shower in peace. I'm asking for ten minutes without you squawking about this being your cottage. Ten minutes, Gabby."

"You know what," I snapped. "I have half a mind to walk in there and brush my teeth regardless of your state of dress. Like you said, I've already seen you naked."

The door pulled open, and he looked at me with his toothbrush hanging out of his mouth. There was a spark of mischief in his eyes. His gaze held mine for several seconds before he turned away. I watched him rinse and spit and then walk to the shower to turn it on. I stood in the doorway with my box of crackers and bottle of water.

Before stepping into the shower, he looked over his shoulder and smirked. "I'm going to start charging if you keep ogling my body."

I glared at him and stepped into the bathroom. I dropped my crackers and water on the counter and reached for my toothbrush. I could be just as calm and cool as he could.

Chapter Twenty

Jake

I couldn't help but smile as the hot water sluiced down my chest. She was so damn stubborn. I knew she was purposely trying to push my buttons. My mistake was letting her push those buttons. Not anymore. I was giving as good as I got. She wanted to be the queen. I got that. Being nice the first week had gotten me nowhere. Now, she was just going to have to deal with my asshole side. I wasn't going to go out of my way to be a jerk, but I was certainly not going to roll over and play dead while she ran over the top of me.

People looked at me and assumed I was this tough guy. I wasn't. I was a damn softie. My parents had raised me to respect women and treat them with kindness. I was taught to treat everyone with kindness. I was the proverbial nice guy, and it was starting to kick my ass. Amanda had taken advantage of my willingness to compromise and bend. She'd used me, and it bit me in the ass. Even with the divorce, she'd taken advantage of my unwillingness to be involved in a long, drawn-out fight.

I hated confrontation. I preferred to live and let live. I didn't like making other people uncomfortable or sad. If I could do something to prevent everyone else from being upset, I tried to do it. This is what it got me. I got caught outside in a storm because the woman I was trying to be nice to took advantage of my kindness. No more. I was putting my foot down. I had no more fucks to give when it came to trying to please her. The other night I had wondered why she was single. She was the total package. She was beautiful and smart and could be funny. But she was also demanding. This snarky side of her would drive away a saint.

I could hear her moving around the bathroom. I knew what she was doing. She was trying to ruin my shower by being obnoxious. She brushed her teeth and was knocking over shit on the counter. Did she plan on waiting around until I got out? Maybe she was hoping for another peep show. I had no problem with her looking at me. I liked that it was about the only way I could disarm her. She was cool as a cucumber all the time, but when I was naked, she got flustered. It was my secret weapon and I planned on using it whenever I could.

I was rinsing my hair when she flushed the toilet. "Fuck," I hissed and jumped out of the stream of water that had turned to straight hot.

She was probably laughing right now. I wasn't going to give her the satisfaction of saying anything more. I suffered through the hot water until it returned to the temperature I had it set at. To piss her off just a little further, I had the hot water up a little higher than my normal shower. My goal was to drain the hot water tank. When she got her sweet little ass in, she was going to get a first-hand feel of what it was like to take a cold shower. She had the benefit of putting on dry clothes afterward.

The curtain was ripped back. "What the hell?"

She was standing next to the shower completely nude. Damn if my body didn't react to seeing her naked. "What are you doing?" I frowned.

"You're determined to use all the hot water, aren't you?" she asked.

"I'm taking a shower," I said. "I've been in here a few minutes."

"The steam is rolling out," she said.

"Go away, Gabby," I said and turned to give her my back.

"Don't act shy now," she said and stepped into the shower behind me. "You've seen me naked. I've seen you naked. It's nothing new. I'm not about to take a cold shower. If you insist on using the hot water, you're going to have to share."

She actually pushed me out of the way and hogged the water stream. "What the hell are you doing?" I asked.

"I'm taking a shower," she said. "Just like I told you I was going to do."

"I'm in the fucking shower, Gabby," I growled. "You cannot possibly decide this belongs to you as well."

"I called dibs."

"I got in first!" I snapped. "Isn't that your whole premise for your argument that the cottage belongs to you? You got to the island first, therefore it's yours. I got to the shower first, therefore it's mine."

I had to keep my back to her. Damn my body for reacting to a naked woman in the shower. How could I possibly be turned on when she was pissing me off? I turned just enough to grab her arm and pulled her out of the way.

"Hey!" she protested.

"I've got soap in my hair," I said. I leaned back and tried to wash the soap from my hair. I could feel her looking at me which was doing nothing to calm the erection budding to life. I tilted my head forward and looked right into her eyes.

"Done?" she asked.

"No, I'm in the shower and I'll take my time."

She reached for the bottle of liquid body soap she'd left in the shower. I watched as she squirted some onto her loofah before she started lathering it up over her body. She was teasing me. I couldn't look away as she rubbed the loofah down one arm, then the other. She ran it over her stomach and between her breasts. This was better than a wet dream. I had no doubt in my mind she was doing it all on purpose. I wasn't even trying to hide the erection anymore.

"I need to rinse," she said calmly.

I nodded with my gaze focused on the bubbles covering her skin. I moved to the side a few inches to let her get under the water. Her soap-slicked body brushed by mine. I got a whiff of strawberries. Her scented bodywash was teasing me. Her back was to me with her face turned up to the spray. I watched her run her hands over her body once again as the bubbles slid down her body and pooled at our feet.

She reached a hand up. "Can you hand me my shampoo please?" she asked.

"No."

"Excuse me?" she turned to look at me.

"Get it yourself," I said.

"Rude," she snapped and reached for the bottle.

I watched her grab it and squirt a puddle in her hand. Without asking, she shoved the bottle back at me. "Can you at least put it back on the shelf? You're kind of in the way."

I took the bottle and put it back on the shelf. Watching her wash her hair was one of the most erotic moments of my life. She scrubbed her scalp with her fingertips before turning around and facing me. Her eyes were closed as she rinsed her hair. There was a lump in my throat as I watched her with her back slightly arched and her breasts thrusting upward. I watched a droplet of water run down her shoulder and between her breasts. The urge to lick that droplet away was powerful.

She reached out her hand again. "Conditioner, please," she said without opening her eyes.

"No."

She stood up straight. Her body was directly under the water. The spray ran down her face, causing her to wipe her hand over her face to clear the water. "Just hand it to me please."

"No," I said defiantly.

"You are such a childish asshole," she hissed and leaned forward to grab the bottle to my left. Her breasts brushed over my arm. If she was purposely trying to tempt me, it was working. She slipped and because I wasn't a total dick, I reached out and grabbed her to keep her from going down. The shower wasn't all that big. If she went down, she was taking me with her.

"Thanks," she murmured, and looked up at me.

I wasn't going to keep playing this game. If she wanted to play with fire, she was going to get burned. I grabbed her upper arms and jerked her against me. I let her feel my erection pressed against her stomach. Her lips parted. I took the chance and kissed her. If she didn't want me, she'd push me away. She could slap me or get out of the damn shower. She didn't do that. I felt and heard her put the bottle of conditioner back on the shelf. A moment later, her hands were sliding into my hair, and she was kissing me back. Her soft body pushed against mine. I dropped one arm around her waist and held her close.

Her soft moans echoed around us. The woman was practically climbing me. I had to reach out and brace myself before she took us both down. She was attacking me. Her nails scored over my skin as her breasts smashed against my chest.

"Slow down," I murmured.

"No. I need this. Right now."

As usual, she was bossing me around. This time, I didn't mind so much. I grabbed her chin and held her steady while I thoroughly invaded her mouth with my tongue. I kissed her until she was clawing at me and begging for more. I had her right where I wanted her. Hell, I had her right where she wanted to be. As much as I would have liked to take her right there in the shower, it was far too dangerous. We were already slipping and sliding.

"We need to get out," I said, even as she was kissing and sucking on my neck. She was hanging off me. Her arms wrapped around my neck and one leg hooked around my thigh.

"No," she said and rubbed her crotch against me. "I want this. Don't try and tell me you don't. I know you want me. I can feel it."

"Babe, I want you, but we're going to kill ourselves if we try any acrobats on this slick floor," I told her.

She groaned and kissed me again. "But it feels so good in here."

"I'll make you feel good," I promised. "Come on. Out."

She wasn't letting go of me. I did the only thing I could do; I hiked her up and carefully stepped out of the shower with her attached to my body. I gingerly stepped to avoid slipping. I managed to dry my feet on the rug before she sprang into wildcat mode again.

Her mouth covered mine and once again, she was grinding her hips against me. I walked a few steps and pushed her against the wall in the hallway. It only took a few seconds to find her entrance. I probed once with my finger to make sure she was as ready as I believed her to be. Then I was pushing inside her. She cried out and slammed her head back with one arm reaching up and the other firmly wrapped around my neck.

"Yes!" she cried out. "Yes, yes, yes!"

I jerked my hips and thrust inside her. Her breasts bounced, begging to be kissed. I bent forward and buried my mouth in her breasts. I thrust as I sucked at her nipples. Her nails scraped down my back once again. I flinched with pain that quickly turned to pure pleasure. The woman was losing her mind. I loved it. I loved that I could drive her mad. I continued to pound into her.

"Don't stop!" she demanded.

I wasn't about to stop. I pushed on until she was crying out pure gibberish. Once again, I felt like I was the man. I made this woman who was normally so damn bossy and stuffy, crazy with ecstasy. Her body collapsed forward with her head resting on my shoulder.

"Feel better?" I asked.

"Mmm, almost," she said and lifted her face to look me in the eyes. "Better, but not good. I'm not done."

"I know," I said, and carried her into the bedroom. "Me either."

Chapter Twenty-One

Gabby

He dropped me on the unmade bed and stared down at me. His chest heaved up and down. The poor man had done the bulk of the work. I sat up and then scooted off the bed with my hand pressed against his chest. I could feel his heart pounding.

"Lay down," I said.

He wrapped his fingers around my wrist and looked me in the eyes. "Why do you insist on being so bossy?" he asked.

I smiled and pulled my wrist free of his hold. "Because I know what I want. Now, lay down. Please."

His eyes were stormy as he turned and sat on the edge of the bed. I pushed against his chest until he was lying on the bed. "Scoot," I ordered.

He grinned. "You could have been a dominatrix."

"I'll keep that in mind," I said as I crawled over him. "I've always thought I looked good in black leather."

"You would look hot in black leather," he growled.

"Too bad there wasn't anything on the island," I said.

"Like?"

"I could really get down with some cuffs," I cooed as I trailed my fingertips around one pec than the other.

"Blindfold," he offered.

I nodded and leaned forward to kiss his chest. "Absolutely."

"Toys?"

I raised my eyes to look at him. "Depends."

I could feel his erection rock-hard against my thigh. I kissed around his naval before sliding my tongue back up to his chest. I adjusted my body over his and prepared to take him back inside me. His eyes were locked on mine as I slowly lowered myself over his thick cock. I took my time impaling myself on him.

He didn't flinch or move a muscle. His hands gripped the blanket. I had to bite my lower lip to keep from crying out once again. He was so damn hard and big. He filled me completely. After already having one orgasm, I thought it would take a while before I was ready for another. My body had other plans. I could feel the coiling low in my belly.

"Damn, woman," he groaned. "Do you know what you do to me?"

"I hope I'm making you as crazy as you made me," I replied.

His hands released the blanket once I was fully seated against him. They rubbed over my thighs and around my waist. "This is the best view on the island," he groaned.

I smiled down at him before leaning forward to brush a kiss over his lips. "You think?"

My hair dragged over his chest, causing him to jerk. That little jerk triggered a series of spasms. I gasped and sat up with my hands pressed against his chest. "Ride me," he growled.

I smiled and rubbed my hands over his chest. "Now who's bossy?"

"It's my turn."

I leaned back, keeping one hand on his six-pack abs and reaching behind me to rest my other hand on his thigh. Everywhere I touched, it was hard muscle. I loved that he took care of himself. He worked hard to maintain his athletic body. It couldn't be easy.

I rolled my hips a few times before slowly grinding hard against him. He groaned loudly with his hands massaging my thighs. "Just like that," he said in a strained voice. "Squeeze me."

I continued to move until we were both gasping for air. My body was wound so tight, I knew it was just a matter of time before I exploded. I sat forward and grabbed his hands in mine before pinning them to the bed on either side of his head. I was in total control. The man below me was at my mercy. I rode him hard. His eyes squeezed shut and his entire body went stiff as a board a moment before he roared like a lion.

The sheer sound of his roar of pleasure was enough to drive me over the edge. I cried out, squeezing his hands while we tumbled into sweet oblivion together. My body spasmed and tightened around him with each shudder of his body. We both jerked and gasped as the sweetest little aftershocks tore through our bodies. I finally collapsed against him with my body draped over his. His arms wrapped around me and held me close.

I was afraid to talk. I didn't want to ruin the moment. It seemed like every time I tried to talk to him, I came off as a judgmental, cranky bitch. I didn't want to be like that. I didn't want to keep pushing him away. My dad's advice echoed through my mind. I could be nice. I had to play nice just a little while longer. It wasn't like I didn't like the man. I did like him. That was the problem. I didn't want to like anyone who was going to end up hurting me. This thing was over in a few short days. I couldn't let it go beyond what we already had.

Instead of talking, I listened to the rain still beating against the roof. It was soothing and made me want to curl up in bed all day. We could sip hot chocolate and... The only other thing we could do was talk or have sex. I knew which one I preferred.

Eventually, I slid off his body and reached down to grab the blankets. My hair was still damp and there was a chill in the air. "Well, that happened again," he said with a small laugh.

"Yes, yes it did," I said with a sigh.

"You're not throwing me out of your bed," he stated.

"No, I'm not. I think it's time we got real."

"What does that mean?" he asked.

"It means I have to confess I'm attracted to you," I said. "You drive me crazy but there is no denying the chemistry between us."

"I agree," he said. "I think we fight because we're trying to deny that chemistry. It makes me cranky."

"Me too," I laughed. "I guess we should just give up on trying to deny there is something happening and just go with it."

"You're okay with that?" he asked.

"I am."

"That works for me," he said, and I could hear the relief in his voice. "We're both supposed to be getting away from the stress back home. I think this week has been just as stressful as it was before I came out here."

"I'm sorry," I said. "I didn't mean to ruin your vacation."

"You haven't ruined it. I suppose my tolerance to bullheaded women is extremely low. You just managed to push buttons that were already raw."

"Ah, so there is a woman back home," I teased. "Bad breakup?"

He scoffed. "You could say that."

"Want to tell me about it?" I asked gently. "If not, I get it. I won't pry."

"I was married before," he finally said.

I sat up a little. "You were married?"

He nodded. "I was."

"How long ago?"

"The divorce was final the day before I came out here," I said. "Not final, final, but we'd both finally agreed to a settlement. Technically, I agreed. She demanded and I agreed."

So much of his attitude towards me made sense. "I'm sorry," I said. "How long were you married?"

"We were together fifteen years, married thirteen," he answered.

"That's a really long time. Was it one of those mutual things?"

He snorted and began to rub my arm. "No. It should have been, but I was a damn fool. I let that woman run roughshod over me for years. Really that's how our relationship started. It just got worse. Things had gone from bad to worse. One day I came home and caught her in bed with another man. She wasn't even sorry for it. I left that day and never went back. I filed for divorce. She got some high-powered attorney and took half of everything. Half of my wealth. She got the house."

"But she cheated on you!" I protested. "That seems unfair."

"That's what my lawyer said," he sighed. "At first, I was ready to fight. I know I could have held on to more than I did. The business was mine. I started it with the money I earned from sponsorships and a few advertising deals. She was my financial advisor. That's how we met. She was this pretty, smart lady paying attention to some dumb jock that didn't know the first thing about investing. She was the one who convinced me to start the business. Looking back, I realize she was just a little baby gold digger. She saw an opportunity and she sank her claws in deep. I thought she truly loved me. I gave her my all."

I couldn't believe it. The poor man. "I'm so sorry," I said again. I didn't know what else to say.

"You don't have to be sorry," he said. "I just thought you should know. I'm not usually this much of a dick. I'm just a little jaded and the littlest things have a way of getting under my skin."

"I get it," I said. "I've been purposely pushing your buttons. I swear I'm not usually like this either. I'll do better."

"Thanks," he said. "I'll do better too. I don't want to ruin this trip. We're stuck here together, and we should make the most of it. Even if we do act like we hate each other, I think there's something under the surface happening."

I nodded and kissed his chest. "There is definitely something happening, but we don't have to label it, right? Can't we just be?"

"Yes," he agreed. "I would prefer it that way. This trip was supposed to be a cleansing of my palate so to speak. I wasn't prepared to be around anyone. When I booked the trip, I was so ready to run away. I came out here because I wanted to get away from everyone, especially one very annoying woman."

I laughed at the poor man's fate. "And then you landed on an island with me. A woman who seems to have channeled your ex-wife."

"Trust me, you're not like her," he said. "Amanda loved to torment me. Even after I moved out, she called me all the time to bitch at me. I was so stupid I actually listened and even apologized."

"How long ago did you move out?"

"A year," he said. "For an entire year I've bent over and let her fuck me every which way because I didn't want to argue. I just wanted to find a way to get on with my life. I was looking for peace. I'm really not the kind of man who likes to argue. I don't like strife. I just want to go fishing or sit in front of the TV and watch a game with cheap beer and unhealthy snacks. When we were together, I had to give up everything I was to try and fit into her world. I came out here as a way to dunk myself in the world I knew I loved. It was supposed to be a cold shock to my system to recalibrate and get me back in tune with who I really am."

"Wow," I said and really felt terrible for the way I had treated him. "You've been through so much. You really did need this vacation. I hope I haven't totally ruined it."

He grinned and pulled me close. "Did I mention the part of being celibate the last year? Okay, that's a lie, there was one woman one time, but it was so not worth noting. The last two years of my marriage to Amanda were just as bad. We had fallen out of love with each other a long time before the end of the marriage. I don't know if she had ever been in love. We rarely had sex and when we did, it was more of a job than a pleasure. You've broken my streak. You made this vacation very, very nice and probably more of what I needed to feel normal again than some fishing."

"Glad I could be of service," I laughed.

"Oh, you have no idea how desperately I needed that exact service," he said. "I feel like a whole new man. Got all the pipes cleaned out and things are good."

I giggled as I snuggled against him once again. "I'm glad that I didn't totally ruin your vacation. Did the fishing help though? I mean, do you feel like you've accomplished what you set out to do?"

"I think so," he said. "It wasn't the idea that I had in mind, but I don't regret any of it."

"Good," I said and felt a little better.

"What about you?" he asked.

"What about me?"

"Are you getting what you needed from this trip?" he asked.

I debated how to answer that question. "I think so."

"You think so?" he questioned. "Is it because I'm here that you can't?"

"No," I shook my head. "Definitely not. It's not you. I'm just trying to figure out how to work through some stuff."

"Do you want to tell me what kind of stuff?" he asked gently. "After all, I opened up to you about my lack of sex."

I smiled up at him. "I don't know if I had to come here to work through my stuff," I told him. "I came here to get away from my life because it suddenly felt like it was crushing me."

"Did something happen?"

I blew out a breath. "My dad died."

"I'm sorry," he said and kissed the top of my head. "When?"

"A couple of weeks before I came out here. It wasn't a total surprise. His health had been failing. It just, well, I wasn't totally prepared for that phone call. He had a stroke and was gone. I never got to say goodbye. I never got to promise him I would be okay. He was in a home because I worked so damn much I couldn't take care of him. Technically, that had been his choice. He didn't want to be a burden, and with his money, he could afford the best of the best. He seemed happy, but I keep thinking, what if I would have been around more? What if I had gone to see him a few days before he died? I might have been able to see the signs and managed to prevent it."

"You can't take on that guilt," he said. "You said he was in a home. I'm sure they had trained staff to monitor his health."

"Yes, but I might have seen something different. It just kind of hit me that I spent all my time working and had ignored the only person in my life that I loved. When he died, I told no one. I took a day off and arranged the funeral. I scheduled the funeral on my normal day off since he wanted to be cremated. I went back to work the next day like nothing happened. No one I work with knows he passed away. I told no one because I had no one to tell. No one that I was close to."

"No friends?" he asked. "I'm sure you work with people who consider you to be a friend."

"They are work friends," I said. "They're not my true friends."

"Maybe they could be if you let them," he said.

"You're right." I nodded. "And that's something I've come to realize since I've been here. I've isolated myself like I was on a deserted island. I bark and snap at anyone who tries to get close because I don't want them in my bubble. I lost my mom ten years ago. It hurt, but it wasn't like this kind of pain. Losing my dad, well, it sucked. I'm officially an orphan. I have no siblings. No aunts or uncles. No one."

"I'm sorry," he said. "I'm especially sorry I was hard on you. My mom always tells me you never know what someone else is going through and to always treat others with kindness."

"You couldn't have known, and I was the one barking at you first."

"Can we agree to start over?" he asked. "We can be friends, lovers, roomies, whatever you want."

"How about we just be. No labels. No rules. We just be what we are. Whatever happens, happens. I'm here because I've been trying to control everything for too long. I have to take a step back and just let shit happen the way it was meant to."

"I can absolutely get on board with that," he said. "Thank you for telling me about your dad. I'm sorry he's gone. I don't know what that feels like, but I know it's coming."

"Don't waste time," I told him. "Visit often. Even if he drives you nuts, visit anyways."

"Good advice," he said, and kissed the top of my head again.

Chapter Twenty-Two

Jake

I took the fish off the hook and added it to my bag. Birds soared overhead. I knew the seagulls were hoping to steal my catch. It was early in the morning. The sun had only been up about an hour, and I suspected Gabby was still sound asleep. The last couple of days had been very calm. We hadn't had sex again since the morning we really opened up to one another.

Oddly enough, I felt closer to her than anyone else in my life. We didn't have to have sex to be close. During the day, we mostly did our own thing. She spent a lot of time walking or reading on the beach. I often did the same, but on the opposite side. At night, I would drift up to the cottage and make dinner for the two of us. I slept outside last night because it was a gorgeous night and I wanted to keep the promise I made to myself to get back to the basics.

It had given me time to think about her and what she meant to me. Despite the arguments we had in the beginning, I cared about her. We had found common ground and it was working for us. It was like we got ten years' worth of fighting out of the way in a week and a half. We were two people thrust into a situation neither of us planned, and there were the obvious growing pains as we learned how to live together.

We were getting along fine, but there was still the situation about who should stay and who should go. Oleg would be coming back in a couple of days. I told her last week I would leave with him. It was up to me to stick to the promise I made. After learning about her reasons for coming to the island, I understood now more than ever why she was here. I may not have thought it was the healthiest choice to be alone, but it was her choice. I was not going to tell her she was wrong. Everyone grieved in their own way, and this was how she chose to do it.

I didn't want to leave, but it wasn't just about leaving the island. It was about leaving her. I wanted to spend a little more time with her. She'd grown on me the last few days. Hell, even when she was shouting at me, I was attracted to her. There was no ignoring the heat between us. We had chemistry. There was something brewing and given a little more time, I was certain it would evolve into something more substantial.

In fact, the way I felt about her was different than anything I'd ever felt before. I was too afraid to call it love, because that felt hasty. But it was something. With Amanda, it had been infatuation. I was a horny kid free of the grueling training regimen I'd been under for most my life. I had broken free and was looking to sow my wild oats. I sowed them with her and once the novelty wore off and I saw her for who she was, my feelings changed.

With Gabby, I had seen the ugly side of her first. Despite the barking and snarky attitude, I saw the good. I saw how beautiful she was on the inside as well as the out. I liked that I got to know all of her before we fell into bed. I desired her for sure, but it wasn't just sex. Gabby was different. If I was brave, I would tell her how I felt. But I wasn't that brave. I was too afraid it would ruin a good thing.

It was best to just let things happen naturally. I packed up my gear and carried my catch back to the fire I had left burning on the beach next to my sleeping bag. The cast iron pan was sitting on the grill over the fire. I quickly prepared the fish and carried it up to the cottage. Fish for breakfast might not be all that conventional, but I was sure she would be thrilled with it. She seemed to enjoy it.

"Good morning," I said when I found her making coffee in the kitchen.

"Oh, what do you have there?" she asked with a bright smile.

"A little breakfast," I said. "If you're up for fish."

"I can't say I've eaten fish for breakfast before, but we're not following any rules here," she laughed. "Should I make some toast to go with it?"

"Sure," I said.

"Coffee is ready," she said as she popped some bread in the toaster.

I helped myself before moving to sit at the table. She buttered the toast, grabbed a couple of plates, and carried them to the table. We dished up and ate our breakfast.

"What do you have planned for the day?" I asked her.

"I was thinking about going back to that little oasis," she said.

I nodded, knowing exactly what she was talking about. I had discovered it on my exploration of the island the first week. "It's nice there."

"Do you want to come with me?" she asked softly.

"I'd like that," I said.

"Unless you had other plans?"

I shook my head. "No plans. I think I've done all I can do in regards to relaxing. I've relaxed. I'm ready to do something other than relax."

"We could run laps around the island," she teased.

"And you know I would beat you," I said with a wink.

"Not fair, considering you're the track star," she shot back.

"I'll give you a three-minute head start."

"I think I would need a fifteen-minute head start and even then, I would fail miserably," she laughed. "Exercise has never been my thing."

"But you're in great shape," I commented.

"Good genes and busting my ass fourteen to twenty hours a day does that," she said. "I should probably start going to the gym. The hospital provides free memberships. I've done a few yoga classes but I'm always so busy. When I do have time, I have to choose between the gym or shopping. Guess which one wins?"

"I don't blame you," I said.

"Do you go to the gym every day?" she asked.

"Are you asking me if I'm a gym rat?" I teased.

"Yes, I suppose I am."

"No, I don't," I answered honestly. "In fact, I rarely go to a gym. I spent the better part of my youth in a gym or on the field. I have a few pieces of equipment at home. I do enjoy running and swimming."

"Do you have a pool?" she asked.

"I do," I nodded.

"But you live in Maine, doesn't it snow a lot?"

"I have an indoor pool," I said. "And an outdoor pool."

Her brows shot up. "Seriously? You must be doing very well at this sporting goods thing."

"Yes and no," I shrugged. "My house isn't a mansion or anything like that. It was on the market for a while. It was a foreclosure. I made a cash offer and I got it for cheap. I've spent the last six months fixing it up. I still have some stuff to do, but it wasn't as bad as the realtor made it out to be."

"You've actually fixed it up or you've hired someone?"

"I've done a lot by myself, but I did hire contractors to take care of the pools. There was a lot of damage done by the previous owner. Now I'm working on cosmetic stuff. Nothing major, but it keeps me busy."

She nodded with understanding. "That's cool. I keep telling myself I'm going to buy a house one day. I just haven't actually done it."

"You live in an apartment?" he asked.

"Yep," she sighed. "A high-rise in the city. It's convenient for work. I never have to leave the apartment on my days off if I don't want to. Everything is delivered to my door. My dry cleaning is picked up. The groceries delivered. It's very easy to be an extremely busy person with that much convenience at my fingertips."

"I remember those days," I said with a shake of my head. "When we first moved out of the city, I will admit I missed the convenience. But with the lack of convenience came the fresh air and roads that weren't clogged with traffic. It's kind of ironic that the house Amanda hated so much and bitched about moving to was the one thing she demanded she take from me."

"That's called being vindictive," she said.

"Yeah, but, whatever. She can have it. I like being away from New York. I especially like not being in the same state as her. It's a little bit of freedom."

"It sounds like you're doing good for yourself," she said. "That's what matters."

"I agree, and I am." I nodded. "I like my life. I like working from my home office. I have a little woodshop on the property. One day, I want to get as good as my dad. For now, I just kind of mess around."

She smiled as she finished her meal. After breakfast, we cleaned up together before setting out to the little oasis that offered a great deal of peace and tranquility. There was a small pond that was filled with rainwater. The trees kept it shaded, which prevented it from evaporating too much. We made ourselves comfortable and actually fell asleep together.

When we woke, it was back to the cottage for lunch. "If you don't mind, I'd like to sleep outside with you tonight," she said.

"I don't mind at all."

I built up the fire and made our bed with my sleeping bag unzipped on the bottom. She carried out a few pillows and a blanket. We sat by the fire and drank wine. I stared at her in the firelight and decided to take a leap of faith. "Oleg will be here tomorrow," I said.

She nodded. "I know."

"I can go if you want me to, or I can stay another week," I said, and tried to gauge her reaction.

She looked at me and I could sense her trying to choose her words carefully. "I think you should do whatever you feel is right."

That wasn't exactly the answer I had been hoping for. All the stuff I'd been feeling was extinguished. She didn't share my feelings. She was okay with us being together on the island for the last week because it was a necessary evil. If she had her choice, she preferred I was gone. I got it. I wasn't going to push anything. Once I left here, it was over. I'd settle back into life, and she would go on with hers.

We crawled under the blanket together with both of us on our backs and staring up at the stars. "It's been good," I said. "I'm glad I stayed the extra week. I feel ready."

"I hope you'll come back and finish your journey," she said softly.

"I don't think it's necessary," I told her. "I think I'm good. If I get any wild hairs, I'll head to Antarctica. I doubt I'll run into any naked strangers there."

She laughed and nudged my arm with her elbow. I was keeping it light to keep from being sad. If I could laugh, I wouldn't feel bummed. I hid my disappointment well. That was something I had learned from my years with Amanda. No one knew what I was thinking most of the time. I smiled and nodded a lot while my heart was shredding on the inside. Same old story.

I woke before her the following morning. I carefully climbed out of the bed we shared and added a few logs to the fire to keep her warm in the morning chill. With one last look at her, I said a silent goodbye and walked up to the cottage. I packed my things and carried my suitcase to the dock. Oleg was unpredictable. I wasn't sure if he would show up first thing in the morning or late this afternoon. I was going to make sure I was ready this time. There was no way I wanted a repeat of our last encounter. She'd damn near taken my head off when I missed the boat last week.

We were playing like we were friends and enjoying our time together on the island, but her non-answer last night made it pretty clear how she truly felt about me being on the island. If I was there, she would deal with it, but if there was a chance I wasn't there, she'd be happier for it.

I sat down on the dock and leaned against one of the posts with my knees bent in front of me. The sun had come up about an hour ago, but the sky was still cast in the beautiful glow of sunrise. On the horizon, I could see dark clouds and wondered if there was another storm coming in. I hoped like hell she was prepared for it. The thought of leaving her alone out here made me a little nervous, but I had to remind myself she was capable. Being alone was what she signed up for.

I wasn't sure how long I had been out on the dock when she walked up.

"What are you doing?" she asked.

"I figured I better wait out here for him," I said. "I didn't want to miss him."

"You're leaving?" she asked, and sat down beside me. "You weren't even going to say goodbye?"

"I figured it would be easier like this," I told her. "No need to drag it out."

"But you're leaving?" She said it as question, which confused me.

"Yes. You made it clear you wanted to get back to your solo vacation. I told you I would leave. I'm a man of my word."

"But I thought you said you might stay," she said, and I wanted to believe I heard disappointment in her voice. But I didn't want to get my hopes up.

"I gave you the choice. You made it clear you didn't want me to stay. I'm not upset about it. I told you I would go, and I will. No hard feelings."

"I didn't say I wanted you to go," she argued.

"You didn't say you wanted me to stay."

She put her hand on my cheek and forced me to look at her. "Stay," she whispered.

"You're sure?" I asked.

"Yes, stay, please," she said. "I'm sorry I didn't make that clear last night. I didn't want to guilt you into staying. You said you had found what you were looking for. I thought maybe you were ready to get back to your life in the real world."

I laughed and shook my head. "Definitely not."

"Let's go back before he does show," she said, and got to her feet. She reached out a hand. I took it and stood facing her. My heart was practically singing at that point. I grabbed my suitcase and dragged it behind me as we headed back to the cottage.

Chapter Twenty-Three

Gabby

When I woke up without him beside me, I panicked a little. I didn't want him to go. Last night I should have told him that, but I didn't. I was too afraid he would reject me. After hearing about his ex and how she manipulated him, I didn't want to do the same. He had to choose to stay on his own. I didn't want to pressure him into anything.

"Sit and I'll make you breakfast," I told him. "I'm not a gourmet chef, but I can make scrambled eggs."

"Thank you," he said and sat down at the table. "Did your mom cook a lot?" he asked.

I burst into laughter. "No. We had a nanny when I was younger. She always prepared the meals. When I got older, my parents hired a cook to come in three times a week. The other days, we usually ordered in. My mom did try to cook on days she was off, but it was just the basics. I never really had time to learn in college. Then I was in med school and working nonstop. It's just so much easier to push a button on a phone and have food delivered to my door."

"I don't fault you," he said. "I only cooked because I had to follow pretty strict diets while I was in training. My parents couldn't afford the chefs like some of my fellow teammates. My mom and I would try out new recipes together. I can make fish and chicken about three million different ways. I swear if I never eat salmon again, it would be too soon."

"I can't imagine a teenage boy on a diet," I said with a shake of my head. "That had to be very difficult."

"It was," he said. "I hated it, but I also knew it was necessary. When my friends were going out for pizza or attending parties and drinking beer,

I used to think about giving it all up. But I pushed on. I started it, and I was determined to finish it."

"That's impressive," I said. "Really, it says something about a guy who dedicate himself fully to training. Why did you stop altogether?"

"I tore some ligaments in my arm after the first meet in the Olympics. I couldn't compete in the second meet. The doctor said the injury was bad enough I would be out for at least three months, possibly longer. He said the chances of me ever reaching the same level I had been at was pretty slim. The trainers and the doctors were telling me how hard I was going to have to work to get back into fighting form if I wanted to make the next Olympics. I just didn't have it in me. It didn't bring me the same kind of joy that it used to. I didn't want to have to bust my ass even harder than I had been. I gave up. I walked away, and I can't say I regret it."

I delivered his eggs and sat down across from him. "I know I would never have the strength or fortitude to do something like that. I think once you have lost the passion for something, there's no point in trying to force it."

He nodded as he chewed. "Exactly. I don't regret quitting. I am almost grateful I tore up my arm. It was the right time. I would have liked to compete in the second meet and try for the gold, but it's in the past."

After breakfast, we were cleaning up when things got heated. One thing led to another, and we ended up in bed together. I was curled against him in postcoital bliss when we heard the sound of the boat. We both stiffened. "Oleg," he said.

I was afraid he was going to jump out of bed and get on the boat. I held him as we both listened to the boat roar closer. Things went quiet. Neither of us moved or spoke. Several minutes later, we heard the boat engine roar to life.

"He's gone," I whispered.

"He's gone," he said. "Here's to another week together."

We laid in bed a while. I felt him relax and not long after, his breathing changed, indicating he was asleep. He was a good guy. I was glad he stayed. I didn't know what was happening between us, but it was real. I had never had feelings for anyone. Not like this. Laying here in bed with him after spending the morning together made me think about a future with him.

Unfortunately, I didn't know if that was in the cards for us. This was one of those scenarios that filled so many movies. Some had happy endings, and some didn't. We were so good together, but we were also very different. I never expected to feel like this about him. About anyone. When I thought he had left this morning, my heart hurt. I couldn't believe I might never see him again. When I found him on the dock, I felt hope. I knew this wasn't going to last forever, but now to think of it ending was just too painful.

On our last full day at the cottage, we decided to take a long walk around the island. He held my hand as we walked in the water. I wanted to bring up the situation that was looming. I wasn't sure how to introduce the topic. We'd been ignoring the end of our vacation for two beautiful weeks. We couldn't just leave tomorrow without talking about what came next.

We sat down on the beach after our long day. I watched him build a fire before he came to sit beside me. He wrapped his arm around me and pulled me close. "Are you sad?" he asked.

"I am. You?"

He nodded. "I am."

"It's been a beautiful month," I said. "I came here with so many expectations, but I never could have expected or planned this happening."

"This?" he questioned.

"Us."

"Me either," he said, and kissed the top of my head. "I'm glad I came and I'm glad I stayed."

"What happens tomorrow?" I asked the question that had been weighing on me for a week.

"Tomorrow Oleg comes, and we leave the island," he said.

"You're dodging the question," I replied.

"I don't know how to answer that question," he said. "Do you?"

"I think it's worth talking about."

"What's talking about it going to do?" he asked. "It changes nothing. We know what happens. You live in California and have a career there. I live in Maine. I have a business and family nearby. I can't pick up and leave. You can't pick up and move. Are you suggesting we try a long-distance thing?"

"I'm not suggesting anything," I said somewhat defensively. "I can't imagine walking away from here and not seeing you again. Are we just not supposed to talk ever again?"

"I think that might be easier," he said. "Prolonging the inevitable seems cruel. It's unnecessarily painful."

"Really?" I asked with surprise. "You're really prepared to walk away tomorrow and not see me again?"

"I'm not saying that's the ideal solution, but I think it's inevitable," he said. "You have been telling me for the last month how busy you are. You work all the time. When are you going to have time for a relationship with a man on the other side of the country?"

He was making a good point. "I don't know. You're just as busy."

"You're right," he agree. "I am, which is why it's a moot point. We are on different paths in life. What we had here is absolutely amazing. I will cherish the memories we've made here together for the rest of my life. You will always hold a special place in my heart."

He was already saying his goodbyes. I felt like someone had their hand on my heart and was squeezing. "This feels like a cruel twist of fate." I sighed. "How do we meet each other like this and then have to part ways? We never should have met. Us ending up here together at the exact same time goes against the rule of chance, yet here we are. I just can't believe this was all for nothing. We spent an amazing month together, and that's all we get?"

"I think so," he whispered. "I don't want to ruin our last night together feeling sad. I want this to end on a good note. I want to wake up in the morning and know that while the time here is over, I'm forever changed for the better. This one of those experiences we have to accept was a blip on the radar of life. We take what we can from it and then we move on."

"You're sure taking this well," I muttered.

He moved to sit in front of me. "Trust me, I'm not happy about this being over. If there was a way to prolong this or for me to move across the country, I would do it in a heartbeat. I would love nothing more than to spend more time with you. I would love to know what could have been if the situation was right. Unfortunately, fate is a cruel bitch."

I pouted, but knew he was right. This was a cruel twist of fate. The song by one of my favorite singers came to mind. Alanis Morrisette said it best. It was horrible to finally get the one thing you thought you wanted only to have it ripped away. I finally met the man of my dreams and although he didn't have a beautiful wife, he did have a beautiful life three-thousand miles away from me.

"Hey," he said, and kissed my cheek. "Let's not let the end ruin our last night together."

I sighed and nodded. "I'm going to need some serious alcohol to get through this night."

He laughed and got to his feet. He helped me up and we headed for the cottage. "What are you in the mood for?" he asked as he stared at the liquor cabinet. "Wine? Scotch?"

"Tequila," I said. "It's a tequila kind of night."

"You got it," he said and pulled out the bottle.

"For dinner, let's keep it simple," I said.

"Works for me. Tuna?"

I rolled my eyes. "You and tuna," I groaned.

He laughed and handed me a shot of tequila. "Just a suggestion."

"How about chips and sandwiches?" I suggested, and took the first of what I hoped was many shots.

"By the fire?" he asked.

"I think that seems fitting," I agreed.

"All right, I'll take the booze and get the fire burning bright," he said, and gave me a quick kiss. "And because I know you think you want tequila; I'm going to bring the wine when the tequila gets to be too much."

"You know me so well," I laughed.

I collected the bottles and put a couple glasses under the other arm before he headed out the door. The moment he was gone, I let the tears fall. I never cried. I hated crying. I was too proud to cry. I hated to admit I was human, but here I was, bawling as I made sandwiches.

I didn't want this to be over. He was the first man I had ever had real feelings for. It was so damn mean to put him in my life and let me fall for him just to have him pulled away from me again. I didn't know what I was supposed to do when I got back. He had ruined me. How was I ever going to find another man like him? I wasn't even sure I wanted a man like him. It would be too hard to have a reminder of the relationship that I had missed out on.

I put the sandwiches and chips in the small picnic basket that was kept in the cottage. Then it was a trip to the bathroom to clean up my face. I didn't want him to see my tears. It would only disappoint him. He was holding strong and wanted to pretend nothing was wrong. I could do that. It was a quick release of emotion.

I pasted on a smile and carried the basket down to the fire he had burning bright. It was dusk with the sun having already made its descent.

"Everything okay?" he asked.

"Yes," I said and put the basket down.

"Tequila or wine?"

I thought about it and decided to go hard. "Tequila," I answered. "I can survive two more shots before I have to switch it up."

He laughed and poured me a shot. "You're going to wake up with one hell of a headache."

"I'll drink plenty of water," I said with a laugh.

We settled in and ate our cold dinner. Neither of us mentioned the impending departure. After getting a good buzz, we decided to head up to the cottage to sleep. The humidity was high, which brought out the bugs. It was that time of year that storms were becoming more frequent, and the bugs seemed to thrive on the humid, sticky air.

"Goodnight," he said as we crawled into bed.

I curled up next to him. "Goodnight," I managed to get out around the lump in my throat.

He fell asleep almost immediately. I thought the tequila would be enough to put me to sleep, but it wasn't working. I kept thinking about tomorrow. There was no way I could walk away from him when we got back to the mainland. I didn't want to. I didn't want to see the sadness in his eyes as we waved goodbye forever.

After a long, sleepless night, I climbed out of bed early. He was sound asleep as I packed up the last of my things. This was probably the coward's way out, but it was the only way I could walk away without my heart totally shattering. I stepped outside and looked up at the cottage. It had only been a month, but it felt like I had lived an entire lifetime in this place.

I slowly walked down the path to the dock. Hopefully, Oleg would spare me the embarrassment of having to look Jake in the eyes after leaving him the equivalent of a Dear John note. If he decided to make this the day he came late, I was going to have to look at Jake again. I couldn't do it. I was barely keeping it together as it was.

Chapter Twenty-Four

Jake

I woke up and reached for her like I did most mornings. I attempted to pull her close when I realized she wasn't in bed. I rolled to my back and stared up at the ceiling. This was it. This was the day I said goodbye to the woman who changed my life for the better. After Amanda, I had convinced myself I was never going to be ready to date again. I couldn't imagine myself ever settling down with someone. I had never imagined loving another woman.

I realized I had never loved Amanda in the way happily married couples loved one another. Amanda and I had a different kind of love. I would have walked through fire for her, but I know she never would have done the same for me. The way I felt about Gabby was all-encompassing. I was afraid to call it love, but I had a feeling that's what this was.

I assumed she was in the shower. I got up and immediately saw the bathroom door was open. "Gabby?" I called out and made my way into the kitchen. It was empty as well.

I stepped outside to see if she was on the porch. It was very rare she was up before me. "Gabby?" I called out again.

I went back inside and that's when I saw the paper sitting on the dining table. My heart dropped. I could already guess what it was. I picked up the paper.

"Jake, I'm sorry to run out, but I thought it would be easier this way," I read aloud. "I don't know where to start. The first two weeks were rough, and I take complete responsibility for that. I'm sorry I was so awful to you. You were nothing but kind and generous. The last two weeks were easily the best time of my life. I will remember my time on the island with you for the rest of my days. Whenever I'm having a bad day, I'm going to think about you running on the beach and seeing me. I'm going to remember that beautiful smile and how happy you looked when you were sitting on the dock with your feet hanging over the edge while you fished. Our time together in front of the fire on the beach will also be a fond memory. Thank you. I don't know how else to say it but thank you so much for making me feel alive again. You've changed my life."

I stopped reading and took a minute to catch my breath. She was killing me with her goodbye. After taking a few deep breaths, I returned to the note.

"I'm sorry to run out, but I thought this would be easier. I'll send Oleg back with the boat to pick you up. Thank you again for showing me such a great time. Take care of yourself Jake. You're a good man. Yes, you are a nice guy, but more importantly, you're a *good* guy. Goodbye, Gabby."

I blew out a breath and closed my eyes. This was not how I wanted the final moments together to go, but I understood her need to get away. She'd said as much last night. I hated that I gave her no hope for a relationship, but I knew it would never work. I couldn't do a long-distance relationship. I wanted all of her. I didn't want her part-time. It wasn't fair to either of us.

Despite me telling her we wouldn't see each other again, I did want to exchange numbers. It was contradictory, but it would leave a door open. Finding her in LA would be like a needle in a haystack. She had never told me which hospital she worked at. I knew she didn't have social media. She was gone. Just like that, gone.

Something snapped in me. I couldn't let her get away that easy. I grabbed my shoes and raced down to the dock to see if she was still there. I was going to tell her I changed my mind and wanted to try and figure something out.

"Gabby!" I called out her name as I broke through the trees. In my mind I was envisioning a sweet reunion. I got to the dock only to find it empty. None of her things were there, which meant Oleg had come and gone. I stomped my foot once. "Dammit!"

Of all fucking days, I had slept through Oleg's arrival. Usually, I was a light sleeper. This was about the worst possible feeling. I went back to the cottage with a heavy heart. I packed my things and finished cleaning up per the rental agreement. I had just put away the last of the books we'd been reading when I heard the sound of a boat motor in the distance. I grabbed my things and shut the door behind me. I walked to the dock and waited for Oleg.

He pulled up and idled the boat while I tied it up. "Good morning," he said with a smile.

"Good morning."

"Your lady friend seemed pretty upset this morning," he said.

"Upset?"

"I had to give her my hanky," he said.

"Damn," I muttered. "I didn't know she was leaving."

"She mentioned that," he said with a nod. "Sounds like the parting wasn't great."

"It was necessary," I said as I climbed onto the boat. "You were playing matchmaker, weren't you?"

He chuckled before bursting into a rattling cough. "I don't know what you're talking about."

"How'd you know?" I asked.

"How'd I know what?" he questioned as he pulled in the rope and started the boat heading away from the dock.

"That we would hit it off?" I asked. "How'd you know?"

"I didn't."

"You took me out to the island and left me there without coming back," I said with a slight hint of accusation. "How did you know we'd get along?"

"I didn't," he laughed. "But I'm not blind. I see two young, attractive people and I do the math."

"What if we were married or with someone else?" I asked.

He laughed again. "I was married once," he said. "My wife would have divorced me if I told her I was going to spend a month alone on an island."

He made a good point. "It was a risky game."

"I'm not a fool," he said. "I saw the signs of some friendly times when I came to drop the groceries that first week. I knocked on the door, and when neither of you answered, I figured it was best not to disturb a good thing."

"Was she okay?" I asked in a somber tone.

He slowly nodded. The boat bounced across the water with the wind blowing against us. "I think she didn't want to leave. I guess that's a sign of a good vacation, when you don't want to leave when it's over."

"I suppose it is," I said. "What's it mean when you've got a broken heart after a vacation?"

"It means you have some decisions to make," he said calmly.

I tried to press him further, but he wasn't giving anything up. We arrived at the dock. "Car's here," Oleg said.

"Thanks," I said. "For everything. I appreciate your matchmaking skills, even if my heart feels otherwise."

He slapped my shoulder. "When you meet a good one, you don't let them get away."

I loaded my bags in my car and climbed in. The ride back into town was very somber. By the time I got home, I had really worked myself into a state of depression I hadn't felt in a long time. Even catching my wife cheating on me hadn't left me feeling like this. It felt like I had lost a piece of my soul and I didn't know how to get it back.

That wasn't true, I knew how to get it back. I just didn't think I could get it back. Her departure had made it clear she wanted to make a clean break. I understood the sentiment. Last night, I had been the one to shut down the conversation about what came next. I wrongly assumed it would make things easier.

After being home for an hour and unpacking my stinky suitcase, it was time to dip back into the real world. I poured myself a stiff drink and went into my home office. I plugged my cell into the charger and turned it on before turning on my computer. All of this could technically wait until tomorrow, but I was hoping to find a good distraction.

As expected, my email box was full. My COO did a good job handling the bulk of the business, but there were still some things I had to deal with. After a month away, there were a lot of things to deal with. Some stuff would have to wait until tomorrow, when I was at a hundred percent. I wasn't there yet.

With the bulk of the emails taken care of, I turned to my phone. My voicemail icon was flashing to let me know it was full. I knew there was little chance that was all work-related stuff. My private cell was reserved for a handful of people.

I put it on speaker to listen while I checked the financials for the company. "Where are you?" Amanda's voice cut through the quiet in my room.

I grimaced and actually shuddered. I quickly deleted it and went on to the next voicemail. "If you're purposely ignoring me, that's not cool," Amanda's shrill voice cut through the room again. "I need to talk to you. This is important."

Once again, I deleted and moved on. "Dammit, Jake," she whined. It sounded like she'd been crying or was drunk. It was hard to say which. Amanda could turn on the tears with very little effort. "I need to talk to you. I'm going to drive my ass to your house if you don't pick up."

I laughed out loud at the thought of her pounding on my front door. I hoped she did. The next three messages were pretty much the same thing. The last one, that one gave me pause. I played it, saved it and replayed it.

"Jake, this is Amanda. You've dodged my calls for almost a month. I tried to do this the nice way. Unfortunately, you've forced my hand. I guess I'll be seeing you in court."

After hanging up the voicemail, I checked my text messages. Most of the eighteen texts I had were from her and all the same. She needed to talk to me. That was code for I want to bitch at you. While I was holding the phone, it rang. No surprise, it was her again.

Because I was in a shit mood and felt like being shitty in general, I answered the call. "What?" I snapped.

"Finally! Where have you been! I've been calling you. You can't just ignore me!"

"Actually, I can," I said. "I told you I was going on vacation."

"And you're going to tell me you didn't take your phone," she spat.

"Yes, actually, I am going to tell you that," I said. "It's none of your business what I do or don't do."

"I wouldn't be so quick to say that," she said with a snideness in her voice I had come to loathe.

"What do you want?" I asked with a sigh. I thought it would be nice to be a dick and take out some of the frustration I felt, but I was rethinking that. She was like talking to a vacuum. I could feel her sucking the soul from my body.

"He left me," she sobbed.

"Who left you?"

"Him! That cheating asshole!"

Now I was suddenly very glad I took the call. "Do you mean the man that you were supposed to marry?" I asked. "The man you were fucking while you and I were married? The man you cheated on me with?"

"Don't be mean," she pouted.

"I'm just trying to understand the situation," I said, and fought back a laugh.

"He was with that floozy from his work," she complained. "I was being so thoughtful and took him his favorite sushi for lunch. I caught him banging her on his desk!"

This time, I did laugh. I quickly stopped, but the reaction had been instinctual. "I don't know what you expect me to do about it." Then a thought occurred, and my blood ran cold. "You're not calling to ask me to stop the divorce proceedings, are you? That ship has sailed. I wouldn't let you back in my bed, my house, or my life if you paid me a million dollars. Not the million you took from me, but another million. Never. I've learned my lesson with you."

"Stop being such an asshole," she snapped. "This is serious. We were supposed to get married!"

"Yes, I heard," I said dryly. "Rumor has it you were planning a big wedding at my house."

"*My* house," she corrected.

"Yeah, whatever. I guess you'll just have to find another victim."

"I'm not sure I can afford the mortgage," she said.

"What the hell are you talking about?" I asked and sat forward. "You fought to get that house. Don't tell me you actually expected me to pay the damn thing off for you? You had to have that monstrosity of a house and the hefty mortgage that went with it. If you can't pay it, I'd suggest you get a second job or sell it."

"I can't," she sighed. "Not until the divorce is finalized in court."

"Don't you dare try and fuck this up, Amanda," I growled. "You got everything you wanted. I'm not paying you another red cent. I'm not giving you anything else. You took plenty. Figure your own shit out. If your man is cheating, that is just karma coming back to bite you in the ass. Call your lawyer. Call a shrink. Call anyone but me."

I hung up the phone and shook my head. That woman was next level. I couldn't believe she actually thought I was going to posse up the money to pay her mortgage. She had already gained a shit load of equity in the house that I had bought. The hell if I was going to make her even wealthier. She could figure out her own mess. I was so done with that woman.

I left my phone in the office and headed for the living room to veg out in front of the TV. It felt like forever since I'd watched the old boob tube. I settled into my recliner and turned on ESPN to catch up on everything I'd missed over the last month. The whole time I watched the TV, I kept replaying my conversation with Amanda. I knew her. Something was up. I had a very bad feeling I wasn't completely done with her yet. She was not going to let me go until she had completely broken me financially and mentally.

THE END

DISTANT SHORES
LEXY TIMMS
DISTANT SHORES
LEXY TIMMS
GET IT ON
Google Play
kobo
Available at
amazon
nook

The Sea Cottage Series

Surging Tide
Distant Shores
Twisting Ocean

Find Lexy Timms:

Lexy Timms Newsletter:
https://www.lexytimms.com/newsletter
Lexy Timms Facebook Page:
https://www.facebook.com/LexyTimmsAuthor
Lexy Timms Website:
http://www.lexytimms.com

Lexy
Timms
BOSS
BOSS
BOSS
Managing
BOSSES
Lexy
Timms
FREE
for a
Limited
Time

Want

FREE READS?

Sign up for Lexy Timms' newsletter
And she'll send you updates on new releases,
ARC copies of books and a whole lotta fun!

Sign up for news and updates!
http://www.lexytimms/newsletter

More by Lexy Timms:

From Best Selling Author, Lexy Timms, comes a billionaire romance that'll make you swoon and fall in love all over again.

Jamie Connors has given up on men. Despite being smart, pretty, and just slightly overweight, she's a magnet for the kind of guys that don't stay around.

Her sister's wedding is at the foreground of the family's attention. Jamie would be fine with it if her sister wasn't pressuring her to lose weight so she'll fit in the maid of honor dress, her mother would get off her case and her ex-boyfriend wasn't about to become her brother-in-law.

Determined to step out on her own, she accepts a PA position from billionaire Alex Reid. The job includes an apartment on his property and gets her out of living in her parent's basement.

Jamie must balance her life and somehow figure out how to manage her billionaire boss, without falling in love with him.

** The Boss is book 1 in the Managing the Bosses series. All your questions won't be answered in the first book. It may end on a cliff hanger.

For mature audiences only. There are adult situations, but this is a love story, NOT erotica.

USA TODAY BESTSELLING AUTHOR
LEXY TIMMS
SIN
SERIES
Payment FOR SIN
Atonement WITHIN
Declaration OF LOVE
LEXY TIMMS
LEXY TIMMS
LEXY TIMMS

A BUMP IN
THE ROAD SERIES
USA TODAY BESTSELLING AUTHOR
LEXY TIMMS
EXPECTING Love
SELFLESS Act
DOCTORS Orders

He groaned. This was torture. Being trapped in a room with a beautiful woman was just about every man's fantasy, but he had to remember that this was just pretend.

Allyson Smith has crushed on her boss for years, but never dared to make a move. When she finds herself without a date to her brother's upcoming wedding, Allyson tells her family one innocent white lie: that she's been dating her boss. Unfortunately, her boss discovers her lie, and insists on posing as her boyfriend to escort her to the wedding.

Playboy billionaire Dane Prescott always has a new heiress on his arm, but he can't get his assistant Allyson out of his head. He's fought his attraction to her, until he gets caught up in her scheme of a fake relationship.

One passionate weekend with the boss has Allyson Smith questioning everything she believes in. Falling for a wealthy playboy like Dane is against the rules, but if she's just faking it what's the harm?

Sometimes the heart needs a different kind of saving... find out if Charity Thompson will find a way of saving forever in this hospital setting Best-Selling Romance by Lexy Timms

Charity Thompson wants to save the world, one hospital at a time. Instead of finishing med school to become a doctor, she chooses a different path and raises money for hospitals – new wings, equipment, whatever they need. Except there is one hospital she would be happy to never set foot in again—her fathers. So of course, he hires her to create a gala for his sixty-fifth birthday. Charity can't say no. Now she is working in the one place she doesn't want to be. Except she's attracted to Dr. Elijah Bennet, the handsome playboy chief.

Will she ever prove to her father that's she's more than a med school dropout? Or will her attraction to Elijah keep her from repairing the one thing she desperately wants to fix?

THE ONE YOU CAN'T FORGET

Emily Rose Dougherty is a good Catholic girl from mythical Walkerville, CT. She had somehow managed to get herself into a heap trouble with the law, all because an ex-boyfriend has decided to make things difficult.

Luke "Spade" Wade owns a Motorcycle repair shop and is the Road Captain for Hades' Spawn MC. He's shocked when he reads in the paper that his old high school flame has been arrested. She's always been the one he couldn't forget.

Will destiny let them find each other again? Or what happens in the past, best left for the history books?

** *This is book 1 of the Hades' Spawn MC Series. All your questions may not be answered in the first book.*

FORTUNE RIDERS MC
BILLIONAIRE BIKER
LEXY TIMMS
Download For
FREE
Lexy
Timms

THE
DEAD OF NIGHT
SERIES
LEXY TIMMS
Abduction
Bribery
Corruption

THE
HEAT OF NIGHT
SERIES
USA TODAY BESTSELLING AUTHOR
LEXY TIMMS
Depravity
Scandal
Disgrace

Don't miss out!

Visit the website below and you can sign up to receive emails whenever Lexy Timms publishes a new book. There's no charge and no obligation.

https://books2read.com/r/B-A-NNL-MHUUB

BOOKS 2 READ

Connecting independent readers to independent writers.

Did you love *Surging Tide*? Then you should read *Just Me*[1] by Lexy Timms!

[2]

We all need somewhere where we feel safe...

After leaving her abusive husband, Katherine Marshall is out on her own for the first time. She's hopped from city to city to avoid the man who made her life a living hell. When it seems she's finally found a new place where she begins to feel safe, she slowly grows confident that her life is looking up. A chance meeting with Ben O'Leary sets her life on a course and her soul on fire.

Ben launched a business that went on to viral success while he was in college, and now as a thriving entrepreneur, he's most interested in maximizing profits. A billionaire living the dream But all that changes when he sets his eyes on Katherine. Things between the two heat up

1. https://books2read.com/u/bP58Q7
2. https://books2read.com/u/bP58Q7

as they fall hard and fast—that is, until she gets an unexpected surprise that will test the strength of their relationship.

You & Me - A Bad Boy Romance

Book 1 – Just Me

Book 2 – Touch Me

Book 3 – Kiss Me

Read more at www.lexytimms.com.

Also by Lexy Timms

12 Days of Christmas
Snowflake Hollow - Part 1
Snowflake Hollow - Part 2
Snowflake Hollow - Part 3
Snowflake Hollow - Part 4
Snowflake Hollow - Part 5
Snowflake Hollow - Part 6
Snowflake Hollow - Part 7
Snowflake Hollow - Part 8
Snowflake Hollow - Part 9
Snowflake Hollow - Part 10
Snowflake Hollow - Part 11
Snowflake Hollow - Part 12
Snowflake Hollow - Complete Series

A Bad Boy Bullied Romance
I Hate You
I Hate You A Little Bit
I Hate You A Little Bit More

A Bump in the Road Series
Expecting Love
Selfless Act
Doctor's Orders

A Burning Love Series
Spark of Passion
Flame of Desire
Blaze of Ecstasy

A Chance at Forever Series
Forever Perfect
Forever Desired
Forever Together

A Dark Casino Romance Series
High Roller

A Dark Mafia Romance Series
Taken By The Mob Boss
Truce With The Mob Boss
Taking Over the Mob Boss
Trouble For The Mob Boss
Tailored By The Mob Boss

Tricking the Mob Boss

A Dating App Series
I've Been Matched
You've Been Matched
We've Been Matched

A "Kind of" Billionaire
Taking a Risk
Safety in Numbers
Pretend You're Mine

A Maybe Series
Maybe I Should
Maybe I Shouldn't
Maybe I Did

Assisting the Boss Series
Billion Reasons
Duke of Delegation
Late Night Meetings
Delegating Love
Suitors and Admirers

BBW Romance Series

Capturing Her Beauty
Pursuing Her Dreams
Tracing Her Curves

Beating the Biker Series
Making Her His
Making the Break
Making of Them

Betrayal at the Bay Series
Devil's Bay
Devil's Deceit
Devil's Duplicity

Billionaire Banker Series
Banking on Him
Price of Passion
Investing in Love
Knowing Your Worth
Treasured Forever
Banking on Christmas
Billionaire Banker Box Set Books #1-3

Billionaire CEO Brothers
Tempting the Player
Late Night Boardroom

Reviewing the Perfomance
Result of Passion
Directing the Next Move
Touching the Assets

Billionaire Hitman Series
The Hit
The Job
The Run

Billionaire Holiday Romance Series
Driving Home for Christmas
The Valentine Getaway
Cruising Love
Billionaire Holiday Romance Box Set

Billionaire in Disguise Series
Facade
Illusion
Charade

Billionaire Secrets Series
The Secret
Freedom
Courage
Trust

Impulse
Billionaire Secrets Box Set Books #1-3

Blind Sight Series
See Me
Fix Me
Eyes On Me

Branded Series
Money or Nothing
What People Say
Give and Take

Building Billions
Building Billions - Part 1
Building Billions - Part 2
Building Billions - Part 3

Butler & Heiress Series
To Serve
For Duty
No Chore
All Wrapped Up

Change of Heart Series

The Heart Needs
The Heart Wants
The Heart Knows

Cottage by the Sea Series
Surging Tide

Counting the Billions
Counting the Days
Counting On You
Counting the Kisses

Cry Wolf Reverse Harem Series
Beautiful & Wild
Misunderstood
Never Tamed

Darkest Night Series
Savage
Vicious
Brutal
Sinful
Fierce

Diamond in the Rough Anthology

Billionaire Rock
Billionaire Rock - part 2

Dirty Little Taboo Series
Flirting Touch
Denying Pleasure
Forbidding Desire
Craving Passion

Dominating PA Series
Her Personal Assistant - Part 1
Her Personal Assistant - Part 2
Her Personal Assistant Box Set

Fake Billionaire Series
Faking It
Temporary CEO
Caught in the Act
Never Tell A Lie
Fake Christmas
Fake Billionaire Box Set #1-3

Firehouse Romance Series
Caught in Flames
Burning With Desire
Craving the Heat

Firehouse Romance Complete Collection

Forging Billions Series
Dirty Money
Petty Cash
Payment Required

For His Pleasure
Elizabeth
Georgia
Madison

Fortune Riders MC Series
Billionaire Biker
Billionaire Ransom
Billionaire Misery
Fortune Riders Box Set - Books #1-3

Fragile Series
Fragile Touch
Fragile Kiss
Fragile Love

Great Temptation Series
The Devil's Footsteps

Heaven's Command
Mortals Surrender

Hades' Spawn Motorcycle Club
One You Can't Forget
One That Got Away
One That Came Back
One You Never Leave
One Christmas Night
Hades' Spawn MC Complete Series

Hard Rocked Series
Rhyme
Harmony
Lyrics

Heart of Stone Series
The Protector
The Guardian
The Warrior

Heart of the Battle Series
Celtic Viking
Celtic Rune
Celtic Mann
Heart of the Battle Series Box Set

Heistdom Series

Master Thief

Goldmine

Diamond Heist

Smile For Me

Your Move

Green With Envy

Saving Money

Highlander Wolf Series

Pack Run

Pack Land

Pack Rules

Hollyweird Fae Series

Inception of Gold

Disruption of Magic

Guardians of Twilight

How To Love A Spy

The Secret

The Secret Life

The Secret Wife

Just About Series

About Love

About Truth

About Forever

Just About Box Set Books #1-3

Justice Series

Seeking Justice

Finding Justice

Chasing Justice

Pursuing Justice

Justice - Complete Series

Karma Series

Walk Away

Make Him Pay

Perfect Revenge

Kissed by Billions

Kissed by Passion

Kissed by Desire

Kissed by Love

Leaning Towards Trouble

Trouble
Discord
Tenacity

Love on the Sea Series
Ships Ahoy
Rough Sea
High Tide

Lovers in London Series
Risking Millions
Venture Capital
Worth the Expense
The Price of Luxury
Exclusive Passion
Sparkling Christmas
Lovers in London - 3 Book Box Set

Love You Series
Love Life
Need Love
My Love

Managing the Billionaire
Never Enough
Worth the Cost

Secret Admirers
Chasing Affection
Pressing Romance
Timeless Memories
Managing the Billionaire Box Set Books #1-3

Managing the Bosses Series
The Boss
The Boss Too
Who's the Boss Now
Love the Boss
I Do the Boss
Wife to the Boss
Employed by the Boss
Brother to the Boss
Senior Advisor to the Boss
Forever the Boss
Christmas With the Boss
Billionaire in Control
Billionaire Makes Millions
Billionaire at Work
Precious Little Thing
Priceless Love
Valentine Love
The Cost of Freedom
Trick or Treat
The Night Before Christmas
Gift for the Boss - Novella 3.5
Managing the Bosses Box Set #1-3
Managing the Bosses Novellas

Mislead by the Bad Boy Series

Deceived

Provoked

Betrayed

Model Mayhem Series

Shameless

Modesty

Imperfection

Moment in Time

Highlander's Bride

Victorian Bride

Modern Day Bride

A Royal Bride

Forever the Bride

Mountain Millionaire Series

Close to the Ridge

Crossing the Bluff

Climbing the Mount

My Best Friend's Sister

Hometown Calling

A Perfect Moment
Thrown in Together

My Darker Side Series
Darkest Hour
Time to Stop
Against the Light

Neverending Dream Series
Neverending Dream - Part 1
Neverending Dream - Part 2
Neverending Dream - Part 3
Neverending Dream - Part 4
Neverending Dream - Part 5
Neverending Dream Box Set Books #1-3

Outside the Octagon
Submit
Fight
Knockout

Protecting Diana Series
Her Bodyguard
Her Defender
Her Champion
Her Protector

Her Forever
Protecting Diana Box Set Books #1-3

Protecting Layla Series
His Mission
His Objective
His Devotion

Racing Hearts Series
Rush
Pace
Fast

Regency Romance Series
The Duchess Scandal - Part 1
The Duchess Scandal - Part 2

Reverse Harem Series
Primals
Archaic
Unitary

Roommate Wanted Series
The Roommate

R&S Rich and Single Series

Alex Reid

Parker

Sebastian

Zane

Saving Forever

Saving Forever - Part 1

Saving Forever - Part 2

Saving Forever - Part 3

Saving Forever - Part 4

Saving Forever - Part 5

Saving Forever - Part 6

Saving Forever Part 7

Saving Forever - Part 8

Saving Forever Boxset Books #1-3

Secrets & Lies Series

Strange Secrets

Evading Secrets

Inspiring Secrets

Lies and Secrets

Mastering Secrets

Alluring Secrets

Secrets & Lies Box Set Books #1-3

Shifting Desires Series

Jungle Heat

Jungle Fever

Jungle Blaze

Sin Series

Payment for Sin

Atonement Within

Declaration of Love

Southern Romance Series

Little Love Affair

Siege of the Heart

Freedom Forever

Soldier's Fortune

Spanked Series

Passion

Playmate

Pleasure

Spelling Love Series

The Author

The Book Boyfriend

The Words of Love

Strength & Style

Suits You, Sir

Tailor Made

Perfect Gentleman

Taboo Wedding Series

He Loves Me Not

With This Ring

Happily Ever After

Tattooist Series

Confession of a Tattooist

Surrender of a Tattooist

Heart of a Tattooist

Hopes & Dreams of a Tattooist

Tennessee Romance

Whisky Lullaby

Whisky Melody

Whisky Harmony

The Bad Boy Alpha Club

Battle Lines - Part 1

Battle Lines

The Brush Of Love Series

Every Night

Every Day

Every Time

Every Way

Every Touch

The Brush of Love Series Box Set Books #1-3

The City of Mayhem Series

True Mayhem

Relentless Chaos

Broken Disorder

The Debt

The Debt: Part 1 - Damn Horse

The Debt: Complete Collection

The Fire Inside Series

Dare Me

Defy Me

Burn Me

The Gentleman's Club Series

Gambler
Player
Wager

The Golden Game
On The Pitch
Respect the Game
All Game
Sweat and Tears
The Final Score

The Golden Mail
Hot Off the Press
Extra! Extra!
Read All About It
Stop the Press
Breaking News
This Just In
The Golden Mail Box Set Books #1-3

The Lucky Billionaire Series
Lucky Break
Streak of Luck
Lucky in Love

The Millionaire's Pretty Woman Series

Perfect Stranger
Captive Devotion
Sweet Temptations

The Sound of Breaking Hearts Series

Disruption
Destroy
Devoted

The University of Gatica Series

The Recruiting Trip
Faster
Higher
Stronger
Dominate
No Rush
University of Gatica - The Complete Series

T.N.T. Series

Troubled Nate Thomas - Part 1
Troubled Nate Thomas - Part 2
Troubled Nate Thomas - Part 3

Toxic Touch Series

Noxious
Lethal

Willful

Tainted

Craved

Toxic Touch Box Set Books #1-3

Undercover Boss Series

Marketing

Finance

Legal

Undercover Series

Perfect For Me

Perfect For You

Perfect For Us

Unknown Identity Series

Unknown

Unpublished

Unexposed

Unsure

Unwritten

Unknown Identity Box Set: Books #1-3

Unlucky Series

Unlucky in Love

UnWanted

UnLoved Forever

War Torn Letters Series
My Sweetheart
My Darling
My Beloved

Wet & Wild Series
Stormy Love
Savage Love
Secure Love

Worth It Series
Worth Billions
Worth Every Cent
Worth More Than Money

You & Me - A Bad Boy Romance
Just Me
Touch Me
Kiss Me

Standalone
Wash
Loving Charity

Summer Lovin'
Love & College
Billionaire Heart
First Love
Frisky and Fun Romance Box Collection
Beating Hades' Bikers
Everyone Loves a Bad Boy
Dead of Night

Watch for more at www.lexytimms.com.

About the Author

"Love should be something that lasts forever, not is lost forever." Visit USA TODAY BESTSELLING AUTHOR, LEXY TIMMS https://www.facebook.com/SavingForever *Please feel free to connect with me and share your comments. I love connecting with my readers.* Sign up for news and updates and freebies - I like spoiling my readers! http://eepurl.com/9i0vD website: www.lexytimms.com Dealing in Antique Jewelry and hanging out with her awesome hubby and three kids, Lexy Timms loves writing in her free time. MANAGING THE BOSSES is a bestselling 10-part series dipping into the lives of Alex Reid and Jamie Connors. Can a secretary really fall for her billionaire boss?

Read more at www.lexytimms.com.

www.ingramcontent.com/pod-product-compliance
Ingram Content Group UK Ltd.
Pitfield, Milton Keynes, MK11 3LW, UK
UKHW022025190726
13853UKWH00005B/2121